What Could Have Been

Written By
Luke Melia

Special Thanks: Erica Melia

Copyeditor: Rachael Mortimer & Kat Humphries

Cover Design: David Anderson

New Oxford Novellas

© Luke Melia 2023

Listen to the writing soundtrack on Spotify:

Prologue: The Waffles

One millimetre is considered to be an inconsequentially small unit of measurement. If a painting is hung one millimetre too far on one side, it will still be admired. If a shirt is cut one millimetre too short, it will still fit perfectly. If a cake is baked one millimetre too shallow, it will still be enjoyed just the same. It's the thickness of a credit card, the width of a sharp pencil point, the height of a few sheets of paper. But for Dale, one millimetre was the veil between the life he had and the one that could have been. For Dale, there was no more consequential a unit of measurement.

That hadn't always been the case. Things used to be simple, back before that holiday, before that boat, before that touch. Back to a time when his biggest worry in life was making sure he got to the cafe in time to meet with his best friend, Anna.

Just a short walk from New Oxford's city centre, down a tired dilapidated alleyway, was Waffle On. The tiny cafe was the only thing on the street left open. It was easy to miss, and even those who spotted it tended to steer clear. Waffles and coffee were the only things on the menu, but that was all it needed. The outdated chalkboard, barely managing to stay propped up on the street outside, shouted about how cheap the place was in poorly drawn bubble letters. It didn't claim the food was *good*, but cheap was exactly what had first drawn Anna and Dale to the place years ago when they were teenagers.

Prologue: The Waffles

They'd known each other for most of their lives, having grown up on the same street. Dale's house was next to what they (and only they) called the *cool field* – the only other field within walking distance was frequented by older teenagers, and as younger kids they knew to avoid it on instinct. So the cool field became their hangout spot, a place they could escape to and focus on nothing but trading stickers and seeing who could do the longest wheelie.

As they got older, their friendship circle expanded beyond just the two of them, maybe even enough to be considered a group, but the bond between Anna and Dale remained something separate, something special. Gradually, the cool field was swapped for the *scary field* and the stickers were replaced by cheap vodka as the duo experimented with the expected habits of adolescents. Neither would say they particularly enjoyed it – it was something their peers did, something seen as a rite of passage, almost. They both knew fairly quickly it wasn't for them.

Instead, the pair moved on to the delights of the city's best (well, *only*) dedicated waffle cafe. They considered inviting their other friends – whenever it came up in conversation, each would watch the other, waiting, hoping for them to back down. They both valued the time alone together, more than they'd ever admit. Waffle On had become their place to relax, away from their families, their friends, the noise of the city. It provided the perfect respite from teenage life. Waffle On was the new cool field.

Prologue: The Waffles

Now, both twenty-two years old and earning their own money, they could afford to splash out on somewhere a bit less... sticky. *Much* less sticky. And yet, neither would ever dream of meeting anywhere else.

They sat, as always, in the window booth overlooking the rest of the street – not that there was much to see out there other than a few boarded-up windows and old rusted shutters. The once-blue cushioned seats of the booth had lost much of their colour and stuffing over the *many* years since they'd been installed.

Anna watched as Dale drowned his waffle in velvety syrup. She'd pushed herself back into her seat out of the potential splash zone – her tan hoodie and bright jeans would've shown up any golden drops that made it her way. It was the same reason her brunette hair had been neatly tucked behind her ears. Dale's relentless pouring was a sight she'd witnessed more times than she could count, and yet the sheer volume still always managed to surprise her. She started to think about how the staff must dread the duo coming in. Whatever small profit they made was sure to be swallowed up by the golden sea that Dale demanded every time. Anna wondered at what point the ratio of syrup to waffle tilted in favour of the former. She concluded it was a jug ago... maybe two. She shook off the familiar disbelief and turned her attention back to the conversation.

"Just think... this could be our last time getting waffles," she joked, watching her friend closely to see if he'd take the bait.

He didn't disappoint.

Prologue: The Waffles

"She's not a murderer!" Dale responded, a little louder than intended, which he realised as he noticed the staff staring.

He pulled down the hood of his deep green sweatshirt to reveal his dark hair. It wasn't shaved, but it wasn't exactly long enough to have any sort of style to it. That was how he liked it. He liked his face clean-shaven for the same reason – it kept him tidy while remaining as low maintenance as possible. That was how he liked life, too.

"You don't know she's not a murderer," Anna continued. "You've known her, what, three months? And now you're going on holiday together?"

Dale kept his gaze focused on his precise pouring, even as he spoke. "You've met Suzanne. She's sweet. Does she strike you as a murderer?"

"She might strike *you*," Anna smirked, "with an axe, in your face!"

Dale chuckled, and that split-second distraction was enough to break him from his syrup trance. He traded the jug for his cutlery, ready to tuck into his breakfast.

"Where did the axe come from all of a sudden?" he asked, attempting to lift the golden mush with his fork.

"I don't know… her suitcase? Where do axe murderers normally keep their axes?"

Dale looked up to meet her eyes. "In the faces of their victims!" he quipped.

"Ha! Very good, Mr Sawyer."

Prologue: The Waffles

Anna signalled the waitress for another cup of coffee. She'd always finish her food before Dale would even begin – sometimes before he'd even turned up. Timekeeping was not his strong suit.

"Has Jak met her yet?" Anna asked, referring to Dale's older brother.

"Only briefly."

"What did he think?"

"Well, he didn't think she was a murderer."

"He's always been a bad judge of character," she shrugged, winking.

"Anyway, you're one to talk!" Dale's eyes darted back to his breakfast. "You and Bob went up to Scotland on what, your third date, was it?"

"That's different…"

"Why?"

"Because it's Bob. One date feels like it goes on for weeks. So our third date was like our twelfth date in Bob years."

"He's so *boring*!" Dale spluttered through a mouthful of waffle.

"He's like a sixty-year-old man in the body of a twenty-four-year-old," Anna joked.

Unlike Dale, who had no idea what he wanted to do with his life, Anna always had a clear vision. She wanted to be a police officer. Her plan after leaving school was simple: take any job she could get her hands on to keep herself ticking over financially while she volunteered as a Police

Prologue: The Waffles

Community Support Officer. Then, as soon as the opportunity presented itself, begin her training as an officer.

It was on one of these jobs, cleaning at a local accountancy firm, that she met Bob. She was nineteen at the time, and Bob was only a couple of years her senior, though his early balding and wider frame made him appear much older. Bob was a man of few words, but beneath the silence lay a deeply intelligent man, wise even. Still, his toneless voice, strict routine-led lifestyle, and the way he was effortlessly content had earned him the (probably unfair) mantle of "boring Bob" between the duo. The two would often joke about him in private, but it was never intended as a slight on his character. In fact, it could be described as admiration. In reality, Anna found Bob anything *but* boring. It was a testament to Anna and Dale's connection that, even with one of them in such a serious relationship so young, it had never impacted their friendship.

"He still took you to Scotland. That's pretty exciting."

"It was to an architecture conference," Anna said, with a dead-straight face.

"No it wasn't!" Dale squinted as he tried to work out if she was being serious. "Wait, was it really?"

"No, not really." She smirked to herself.

There was an almighty clink as Dale dropped his cutlery onto the plate, proud that he had polished off his sugar-drenched mountain. There wasn't a single spot of syrup left on the plate. There never was, and it still amazed Anna every time.

Prologue: The Waffles

Dale leaned back into the booth and looked at his friend as she wrapped her cold hands around her roasting coffee cup.

"So, how are you guys, really?" he asked.

"Me and boring Bob? We're…" A different sort of smile spread across Anna's face, a sweeter one. "We're solid. You know, it's… wonderful." The smile quickly reverted back into a cheeky grin. "I mean, he's never tried to kill me with an axe, at least."

"Neither has Suzanne!"

"Yeah, but you might not be able to say that in a few weeks," Anna chuckled, raising her eyebrows. "Been nice knowing you Dale, that's all I'm gonna say."

Part 1
The Holiday

1.1: The Island

It was the summer of 1995, and the Greek sun beamed down on the beautiful island of Corfu. Well, it was the same sun as the rest of the world, of course, but every Brit knows it feels different abroad. Each year during the holiday season the idyllic vista became awash with tourists, all baring pale flesh ripe for tanning (or burning). This year, though, there was one visitor who refused to adhere to the expected attire.

It was Dale's first time in Greece and he was never one to show much skin, no matter the weather. He relaxed on a sun lounger outside the resort where he was staying with Suzanne, his girlfriend of only a few months. Even with the giant parasol overhead keeping him in shade, his legs were sweltering under his jeans – they had been since the moment he stepped off the plane, but it was something he was learning to live with. On top he wore a short-sleeved white T-shirt, and the lack of his usual hoodie was his idea of a summer wardrobe. It was still within reach, though, rested carefully on the table beside him like some sort of security blanket.

He watched Suzanne in the pool only a few feet away, her golden hair floating on the surface, the water so still that it preserved the view of her tall, slender body. Her arms leant against the edge, her legs slowly fluttering in the water to keep her afloat.

"It's a million degrees and you're still in jeans," she said, her tone playful but betraying a hint of disapproval.

1.1: The Island

They'd been in Greece for a couple of days now, and she'd assumed that at some point Dale would succumb to the heat and throw on something more appropriate. She was still waiting.

"It's thirty-five degrees at most," Dale replied, slightly more defensively than intended.

"Yeah, which is damn hot, Dale! Why don't you get in here with me? The water's beautiful."

"I'm looking after our stuff."

He knew it was a weak excuse. Suzanne was the only person in the pool – most of the guests of the adult-only resort had gone out for the day. The only other person in sight was a man sleeping on a grassy patch on the opposite side. He'd been in the shade when he first drifted off, but now was fully bathed in burning light. Dale had thought about waking him a few times but had yet to find the courage to do so.

"Anyway, stop changing the subject," Dale continued. "Are you going to answer or are you going to buy me lunch?"

"Fine!" Suzanne thought back for a moment, trying to remember exactly what he'd asked her. "I'd go... being able to fly. I'd use it to see the whole world, maybe try and find an island that's never been discovered. I'd call it Suzannelane... Suzaland... Suzland... I don't know, something like that."

"Really? But think of all you could do with invisibility!"

"You'd just use that for something pervy!" Suzanne laughed, winking at him.

1.1: The Island

Dale smiled cheekily, ensuring she'd noticed. "I'd use it to hide whenever you wanted someone to watch *Neighbours* with."

"Oh please! You like it just as much as I do." Suzanne playfully flicked water at her boyfriend. He tried to dodge and failed. It was almost enough to get him to move from underneath the shade... almost.

"Right, my turn..." Suzanne said as Dale dried his face.

Her mouth opened, but no words came out. Dale could tell she had something on her mind and was second-guessing herself about asking it.

"Go on," he prompted, "you can ask me anything."

"Your brother, Jak, he's been in a wheelchair for four years, did you say?"

"Five."

"Five years. So since you were seventeen. What was that like? I mean, that's a difficult age anyway, but going through something like that must have been tough. I know for Jak it must've been awful, but what was it like for you?"

"Wow, Suzanne," he said, wobbling his head as if trying to shake off the seriousness of the question. "I asked you about superpowers and you came back heavy!"

"It's fine, you don't have to answer if you don't want to..." She was sincere, but it didn't last, and she once again threw him a playful wink. "You can just buy me lunch instead."

"No, it's fine. It's just not something I've really thought about, I didn't even really have a chance to think about it

1.1: The Island

when it happened... Afterwards, Jak was angry at the world for a long time. My mum had to do a lot of work around the house so he could get around. I helped where I could, I stayed out the way where I could. It was just... a tragic thing that happened. I knew I felt bad for him. Everywhere I went people kept stopping me and passing on their best wishes, telling me how sad it was. But I didn't really process it, I guess. I knew things would be different after that, but I just sort of adjusted. I don't know. That probably sounds cold."

"It doesn't," Suzanne reassured him.

Dale had maintained eye contact throughout their exchange. He'd never shown much emotion to Suzanne (and never did much to anyone, she suspected). She'd never seen him particularly angry, or loving, or sad. For the first couple of weeks of their relationship, she wasn't even sure he was that interested. Gradually, though, she was learning to recognise how he showed affection. The holiday had been his idea – surely that was a good sign? Even as he'd spoken about his brother his tone was matter of fact, like he was reciting from a script. In all their time together, he'd barely spoken a word about how he felt about anything. She'd assumed it was because he was uncomfortable discussing his thoughts and feelings, but now she realised that wasn't it. Maybe he just wasn't somebody who spoke about it uninvited. He didn't seem to mind being asked. She made a mental note of that – she should ask him more.

Dale continued, "Anyway, I was lucky to have Anna there. Jak didn't leave the house for months... maybe even a couple of years, I'm not sure. Mum had nobody to talk to

1.1: The Island

outside of the family, really, but I had Anna. She helped me process it, kept me anchored."

"I'm glad."

Dale considered Suzanne for a second, trying to read her. They hadn't been together long, and he knew from past experiences that having such a close bond with his best friend could create issues with new romances. If Suzanne had any sort of problem with it, then she'd never let it show. He was grateful for that.

"Right, my turn," Dale declared playfully, "and I'm gonna get you back!"

"Bring it on!"

The corners of Dale's mouth started to lift as he thought back to something that he knew would get a rise out of her, something she had tried to hide.

"Remember when we went to your parents' house? Your sister made some comment about breaking your playboy, but you quickly shushed her out of the room. What was that about?"

Suzanne's face turned bright red, even redder than the roasting back of the guy sleeping on the opposite side of the pool. They really should have woken him by now... She climbed out of the water and grabbed the towel beside Dale.

"Come on," she said, "let's go for a walk. I'm buying lunch."

The journey into town was barely half a mile, but the young couple took their time, meandering along the shoreline. They

1.1: The Island

focused on enjoying the warmth of the sun, the smell of the sea, and the feel of the sand beneath their feet. Well, Suzanne could feel the sand, anyway – Dale stood out like a sore thumb walking along the beach in his jeans and trainers, his hoodie thrown over his shoulder. Suzanne, on the other hand, fit right in. Her cream shorts and matching bikini top were a strategic choice, the contrast making her skin look more tanned.

"I was like six years old, and I'd spent all day building a Playmobil town," Suzanne said.

"That's a big commitment when you're six."

Dale wanted to take her hand as they walked, but his palms felt uncomfortably clammy and it was too early in their relationship to subject her to that.

"Right!" Suzanne agreed. "Anyway, Elizabeth was nine, and she was such a brat. She was showing off in front of her friend and she kicked over my veterinary building!"

"No!" Dale gasped, playfully overdramatic.

"Oh yeah, on purpose too! I burst into tears, like my face was just flooding, and I went running to Mum. Elizabeth sprinted after me, trying to calm me down, knowing she'd get in trouble. I ran into the living room, Elizabeth right behind me, along with her friend. And I shouted—"

"Oh no..." Dale said, joining the dots.

Suzanne looked down at her sandals as they glided in and out of the warm golden sand. "Oh yes. I shouted, 'Elizabeth just broke my playboy'."

1.1: The Island

Dale burst out laughing, jokingly bumping into Suzanne as he did.

"It's been like eighteen years since then!" Suzanne grumbled, ignoring her boyfriend's chuckling. It was the most she'd ever heard him laugh. She continued, "I'm a professional sportswriter. I earn more now than either of my parents ever have. And yet, as soon as I step through the door of their house, I'm just the girl that accidently said playboy instead of Playmobil."

"How did you even know what a playboy was?"

"I didn't! I don't know where it came from, it was just an unfortunate slip-up. But now I have to relive it constantly. If we…" – she caught herself – "if *I* ever get married, I'm not letting any of them do a speech as I know they'll bring it up the first opportunity they get. In fact, they may not even get invited."

The couple sat in the outdoor area of Iremia Prin, a cafe-bar in the town. The large awning overhead was doing little to ease the heat. The temperature was at its peak, and for the first time since they got there, Dale was starting to envy those who were comfortable enough to walk around wearing so little. After sharing a lamb kofta salad, which was much spicier than either of them had anticipated, they ordered dessert – the coldest thing the cafe-bar offered. Suzanne had a cone of bubblegum ice cream mixed with raspberry sorbet. Dale had chosen a simple scoop of vanilla ice cream, sitting atop a waffle. The latter was significantly flatter than he'd expected, more like a biscuit. It was no Waffle On, that

1.1: The Island

was for sure. His disappointment intensified when he discovered they didn't have syrup – he looked forward to complaining to Anna about it when he got home.

Conversation had paused while they raced to beat the steady melting of their desserts. Suzanne finished first, unsure where more of it had ended up: on her fingers, the table, or her bare stomach. After trying and failing to dry her fingers with a napkin, she broke the silence.

"I feel like I've told you a lot of embarrassing stories about myself today. You must think I'm such a weirdo."

"Mmm..." Dale mumbled through his biscuit-waffle, "maybe a little."

"Shut up," Suzanne said, smiling. "You've gotta tell me something weird about you, now."

"Like what?"

"I don't know. Some story about when you did something stupid, or something odd you do that nobody knows about..."

"I don't think I have anything," Dale shrugged, taking the last bite of his lacklustre biscaffle.

"Oh, the Mr Perfect act! Don't want to show your girlfriend that maybe you're a flawed human being too?" She meant it good-naturedly, but immediately worried it'd come across sharp.

Dale thought for a moment – not to find something to say, but to decide whether to say it. "I mean – and I've never told anybody this, except for Anna – but sometimes I take things."

1.1: The Island

"Take things?"

"Yeah. Like at the reception desk of our resort. They've got a bunch of stuff, right – the books of matches, those pinecones, the pens with a picture of the island on that people use when they sign the check-in forms? Well... I've got three of those pens in my back pocket."

Suzanne looked him in the eye, puzzled, trying to work out if he was telling the truth. "Show me."

Dale reached into his pocket, pulled out the pens and placed them on the table. He didn't say a word.

"So, you stole them?"

"Borrowed..." Dale corrected, only adding to her confusion. "I'll put them back later."

Suzanne giggled, unsure what to make of it. "What?"

"I don't know. It started when I was maybe seventeen or eighteen or something. I would take things from friends' houses, just things I knew they wouldn't miss. Then next time I was there I'd return them. I guess I got a kick out of knowing that object had gone on a journey, and only I knew about it. Some weird power thing maybe... I don't know."

A broad grin broke out on Suzanne's face.

"Why are you smiling?"

"Ha! Because you're a freak!"

"Well," Dale said, matching her smile, "I guess we're just a couple of weirdos."

"Hey, don't lump me in with you. You're way weirder."

The two laughed together. At some point during the exchange, although neither of them were sure exactly when,

1.1: The Island

they'd stretched their hands across the table to meet in the middle, holding each other firmly. To an onlooker, it would be obvious that this young couple were still in that early phase of getting to know each other – new enough that the passion and excitement were still strong, but just long enough that they were starting to settle into their natural selves around each other. The two took a moment to just appreciate where they were, and who they were with.

The blissful peace was disturbed as they were approached by a toned young man wearing a fluorescent orange cap, the tightest orange shorts either of them had ever seen, and nothing else. That included no shoes, and neither of them was sure how his feet weren't on fire from the burning stones of the pavement. He held a stack of promotional leaflets.

"Hey, you beautiful couple!" the man said with painfully exaggerated enthusiasm.

Suzanne rolled her eyes at Dale, realising their moment of peace was over. She released his hands and they both turned to give the newcomer their full attention.

"How are you two? Where are you from? Are you enjoying Corfu? It's a wonderful island, right? Where are you staying?"

The man didn't give them a second to answer, trying to be friendly while still rattling through his script at a ferocious pace.

"We're good, thanks," Dale said, as dismissively as he could. Not that it made any difference.

1.1: The Island

"Ah, you're English! I love London!" The man thrust a leaflet into his hands.

On the front was a logo for a company called Sotiria Adventure, along with poorly assembled stock photos of people doing various high-adrenaline activities.

"Quad bikes, you like quad bikes? They're fast. We go to a beautiful island, and you can spend all day riding. We eat some fish. It's a paradise. You like quad bikes, yes? Tomorrow, we go."

Suzanne's eyes lit up as she unfolded the leaflet to see a photograph of a bike riding along a dirt path surrounded by lush green trees. The details were sparse; it had a map of the town with a drawn red circle showing where their booth was located, but no details on price. These things never did; it was up to their agents to get the best price they could – something Dale and Suzanne had learnt the hard way.

She held it up to show Dale. "This actually looks really cool," she said, excited by the idea of doing something a little risky.

Although usually risk-averse, Dale summoned up some false enthusiasm – he didn't want his relatively new girlfriend to think he was boring.

"Yeah... yeah, this could be fun," he lied. He suddenly remembered something, but instead of allowing his face to show the relief he felt, he made a big show of feigning disappointment. "Oh Suzanne, we've got that boat trip tomorrow."

"Oh shit, yeah." Suzanne had forgotten all about it.

1.1: The Island

The two of them had booked it on their first night at the resort, with the first agent to approach them. At that point they would have said yes to anything, though they knew now they had paid well over the odds for it.

"No, no!" the man shouted. "A beautiful couple like you don't want to be on some boring boat, you want to be with me, on a quad bike! Come on, think about it, you know, you know!"

"What do you think, Dale?"

A part of him was starting to come around to the idea. Maybe it was the sun making him light-headed, or because he could see how excited Suzanne was at the prospect. Not wanting to disappoint her ranked *just* above not wanting to go on the quad bikes. He reached across the table and took her hand again.

"If you wanna go for it, then let's forget the boat and do this."

She thought about it for a few moments. The brochure said this ran once a week, and they'd be home by the time it ran again... but they'd spent a lot of money on the boat trip, and it'd be a waste if they cancelled now. The man's relentless sales pitch continued in her ear as she did her best to ignore it.

"I think we should do the boat," she said, although her tone remained uncertain. "Yeah. Yeah, Dale, let's go on the boat trip." She was more convincing the second time.

"You sure?" Dale asked, trying to read her.

She nodded. And she was sure – a day relaxing on a boat together meant they could talk, and laugh, and get to

1.1: The Island

know each other more. That's exactly what the holiday was for, to strengthen their connection. The boat would be perfect for that.

If only she had known the impact of that decision.

1.2: The Boat

Getting out of bed the next morning proved difficult. It wasn't a lack of excitement for the boat trip – on the contrary, the idea of spending the day out at sea relaxing in the sun felt like exactly what they both needed. But sleeping in the heat, especially when mixed with the passions of a young couple, was taking them some time to adjust to.

Dale and Suzanne were running later than planned. The icy water of the shower stung on Dale's shoulders; he knew he'd caught the sun, but the tenderness revealed they were much more burnt than he'd realised. He felt betrayed. He'd spent the last few days constantly sticky from his strict regime of sunscreen and aftersun, peeling his clothing away from his skin every few minutes to allow air to reach his body. He hadn't felt truly clean since they'd left home, yet he'd still managed to get burnt. *Bastard sunscreen, bastard sun*, he said to himself. He spent longer in the shower than intended, convincing himself that the cold water would help soothe the burn, but deep down he knew it was too little, too late.

As he suddenly realised the time, he hastily tugged on his jeans and draped a towel over his shoulders. Suzanne was already dressed and ready, wearing a light and loose peach throw with matching shorts over her bikini. Dale made sure she was watching, then smiled and pulled down the waist of his jeans to reveal his swim shorts underneath. Her face lit up; she'd spent all night trying to convince him to

1.2: The Boat

wear them so they could swim in the sea. He was adamant that he wasn't going to, and she didn't want to push it.

They left the resort and rushed to the shoreline. The boat, a small, sky-blue tourist vessel with the name *αλλο* etched onto the side, was ready and waiting. After greeting the overenthusiastic staff and putting their shoes into a box beside the walkway (the staff insisted on this before boarding, something Dale hadn't anticipated – wearing socks and trainers had been a mistake), the couple made a beeline for the top deck. The lower deck was full of families, but the kids weren't allowed to go up the ladder. It was the adult-only deck that had sold the couple on this particular trip. It wasn't that they didn't want to be around the others, they just liked the idea of being away from the noise and only around other adults.

They were relieved to find there was plenty of room for them on the upper deck. They were more relieved when they noticed a free spot under the shade of the fabric covering suspended overhead. They stepped over a sunbathing man, placed their towels in their corner to claim ownership, then settled down quietly together. They weren't quite sure what the etiquette was on excursions like this, but luckily the others aboard took the initiative to introduce themselves.

The first of three other pairs was an older British couple. They were tucked away in the opposite corner, safely under the shade. They must have been in their late fifties, maybe early sixties, and had an easy familiarity with the staff on the boat. They introduced themselves as Reg and Moira the

1.2: The Boat

second that Dale and Suzanne were settled. They explained that they'd been frequenting this part of Greece for over twenty years and correctly guessed that Suzanne and Dale were first-timers.

The second couple was a pair of young men with thick eastern-European accents. They were perched *just* inside the shade, as if they wanted to be able to switch positions to lie in the sun with minimal hassle. Dale heard their names, twice, but they fell out of his head as soon as they left the air. He couldn't ask them to repeat them a third time. Instead, he just referred to them as "the guys" to Suzanne. They introduced themselves as brothers, but Suzanne suspected that wasn't the case. Had it been a mistranslation on their part? Or were they not comfortable using the term *couple* in a foreign country? She wasn't sure.

Last was another British couple, around the same age as Dale and Suzanne. The guy lay confidently on his back in the sun, wearing nothing but a tiny pair of shorts and reflective sunglasses. He was clearly proud of his body, and his chiselled abs backed him up. He was clean shaven, his hair well groomed – this was someone who took a lot of pride in his appearance. His girlfriend lay next to him, on her front, wearing shorts and a bikini top that she'd released the clasp of to allow her full back to be bathed in sunlight. She had her nose in a book. Dale couldn't make out the title, but the cover image looked like some sort of crime thriller. Once the others had finished their introductions, the woman placed the book upside down on the floor to hold her page and contorted her arms around her back to clip her bikini. She then proceeded to sit up and adjust her dark curly hair,

1.2: The Boat

presumably to ensure it was still as it should be after lying in the sun for so long.

"I'm Heather," she said, before kicking her boyfriend on the floor.

"Lyndon," he shouted, without moving a muscle.

"Hey. I'm Suzanne, this is Dale."

"Oh, you're British too," Lyndon said, as still as a statue. "Whereabouts you from?"

Dale left it to his girlfriend to handle the small talk; he knew she was much better at it than him.

"New Oxford. What about you two?" Suzanne asked.

"No way, us too!" Heather blurted as she picked her book back off the floor. "What a small world."

Dale smiled and nodded, just enough to cover the basic pleasantries.

The small talk continued a little – they found out that Heather was twenty-four, Lyndon twenty-nine, and they'd been together for four years. It was little compared to Reg and Moira, who had over four decades together. As talk moved to where each couple was staying, how many times they'd been before, how much they were enjoying their holidays, Dale and Suzanne found the opportunity to fade out their contribution and fall back into their bubble. Their exciting, new, and comfortable bubble. They'd been less forthcoming than the rest, but nobody seemed to mind. The other couples had a sort of combined confidence, like each was able to feed from the other. Dale and Suzanne weren't quite there yet; for now, they were happy to keep to

1.2: The Boat

themselves. Plus, looking around at the others was making Dale feel self-conscious about being overdressed. He told himself that he'd pluck up the courage to take his jeans off and relax in his swim shorts (well, pretend to) before the day was over.

Suzanne curled up and rested her head in her boyfriend's lap, her muscles softening as she relaxed into him. Her warmth, coupled with the sun, made the heat almost unbearable for Dale, but he didn't say a word. She was comfortable, and he liked having her close.

"You better not let me snore in front of these strangers," she whispered.

"Don't worry, they'll just think it's the boat's foghorn."

Suzanne playfully slapped his leg without opening her eyes.

The boat rumbled and pulled away from the dock. Within minutes, they were surrounded by luscious, crystal-clear water on every side. The resort quickly shrunk to a pinpoint on the horizon. Dale could hear the occasional mumblings of polite small talk from the other couples and a constant cacophony of overlapping shouting from the children below, but looking out at the tranquil sea, with his girlfriend resting soundly on his lap, presented a moment of true peace. The gentle rocking of the boat, the graceful dance of the waves… it was almost enough to put him into a trance, and the more he stared, the lower the volume around him became. He wasn't sure he'd ever felt so… nothing. But a pleasant nothing. The moment was broken by a pressure on his

1.2: The Boat

ankle. He looked down to see Suzanne squeezing it; she was awake and staring at him.

Wait... *everyone* was staring at him.

"You there, Dale?" Suzanne asked.

"Yeah, sorry, miles away..."

Dale noticed one of the staff standing at the top of the ladder.

"Do you want a drink?" Suzanne whispered.

Dale connected the dots – the staff member was taking everyone's orders.

"No, thanks," Dale said instinctively, before realising that actually a drink was exactly what he needed. "Wait, could I get a coke or something?"

"Of course," the guy said before disappearing towards the bottom deck. Dale had been the last to order.

After about half an hour of sailing, the boat reached a tiny golden island housing only a couple of shacks. This was their first stop. There was an excited rumbling of shifting feet from the deck below.

"Should we move?" Suzanne asked, unsure why none of the other couples had reacted.

"I don't know," Dale replied.

Lyndon, the ripped British man still sunning himself, shouted over to them, "Nah, this is just an ice cream place for the kids."

"Get us a lolly, babe." Heather nudged her boyfriend with her foot.

1.2: The Boat

Lyndon jumped to his feet so fast that a blink would've missed it. This was the first time he'd moved since the boat left shore.

"Yeah, alright," he said, reaching down into his bag and grabbing some cash. There was a distinct Lyndon-shaped sweat patch where he'd been lying.

"Anyone else want anything?" he asked.

"No, thank you," Moira said.

"I might stretch my legs," Reg replied as he stood up, much more slowly and with more care than Lyndon had. The two of them climbed down the ladder and walked towards the island.

The eastern-European guys followed, but instead of heading to the island, they dove from the bottom deck into the water for a swim.

"Do you want an ice cream?" Suzanne asked, finally moving from Dale's lap.

"I'm good."

Suzanne ignored him, standing up and reaching out her hand. "Since when do you turn down ice cream?" she joked as she lifted him to his feet.

Dale wasn't sure if she actually wanted to go, or just knew that he really did want one, but he was grateful either way. The two left the boat, walked onto the island, and joined the long queue of excited children.

After getting a couple of strawberry cones, Dale's coated in bubblegum syrup, they slowly wandered back towards the boat, taking their time to soak in the beauty of

1.2: The Boat

their surroundings. Save for this tiny spot of sand, there was nothing but gorgeous ocean and pure blue sky as far as the eye could see.

Finally, they made it back and had to join another queue. The staff were stopping all the kids from getting on the boat until they'd finished their ice creams. They were using a bucket to wash their hands before allowing them back on board. Luckily, that rule didn't apply to the adults, as they discovered when the staff waved them past the line.

As they climbed back onto the top deck, they heard the sound of laughter from the guys. Heather was sitting up on the side of the boat finishing her ice lolly. Lyndon was by her feet, a mischievous smile across his face. They didn't hear the words, but they got the context; he'd obviously made some joke about Heather, which the guys had found hilarious.

Dale and Suzanne shuffled past the group and back to the safety of their corner, both focused on finishing their treat.

"You're one to talk. God forbid anyone gets in the way of you and your tan," Heather said playfully, smiling along with the others. "You've spent all day on your back!"

"Sounds like you on our third date." Lyndon winked.

The guys exploded into laughter again. Even Reg joined in, much to Moira's disapproval.

"Don't encourage him," Moira said, elbowing her husband.

"I don't remember that," Heather said. "But they do say we learn to block out *unsatisfactory* memories."

1.2: The Boat

The more the guys laughed, the more it spurred them on.

Heather finished her lolly while waiting for her boyfriend's inevitable retort. When she was done, she scanned her surroundings for a bin.

"What did you do with your stick?" she asked Lyndon.

"In the sea," he responded, while laying a towel over his previous sweat patch, ready to resume his position.

"You didn't, did you?"

"Yeah..." Lyndon stood up, looked over the side of the boat, and pointed. "There it is."

Heather followed his finger, looking over her shoulder to the sea below. As she did, Lyndon grabbed her feet and pushed her overboard. There was a piercing scream, an almighty splash, and an explosion of laughter from the guys.

After a few seconds, a voice shouted from below. "YOU PRICK!" Heather screamed, followed by "Sorry!" when she realised all the kids were looking over the side to see the cause of the commotion.

Lyndon could barely breathe as he peered over the edge and watched the staff help his girlfriend back onto the boat. She rushed back to the top deck to confront him.

"Sorry, babe..." Lyndon said insincerely.

She jumped and wrapped her arms around him, trying to get him as soaked as she was.

"You're such a twat," she said playfully, as she let him go. "I'll get you back."

"Looking forward to it."

1.2: The Boat

"Just for that, you can get me a cigarette." Heather returned to the side of the boat for a second, before realising how easy it would be for him to push her off again. She thought better of it and moved back to her towel instead. Lyndon searched the bag for a moment before throwing her a cigarette. She put it between her lips, then tapped each of her pockets in turn. Her face fell as she came up empty, realising that her lighter had been lost to the sea.

"You moron…" she said to Lyndon, looking overboard for any sign. "My lighter was in my pocket, now some fish has probably got it."

"Didn't you bring a spare?" Lyndon searched deep into the bag.

"Funnily enough, Lyndon, no. I didn't think some idiot was going to push me into the bloody ocean." Heather turned her attention to the other couples on the boat. "Sorry about him… I don't suppose any of you have a light, do you?"

"Sorry," the guys said.

The older couple shook their heads.

"We don't smoke, sorry," Suzanne said, happily tucked away in the corner watching it all unfold.

"Fuck." A disappointed Heather removed the cigarette from her lips.

"Wait…" Dale reached into his back pocket.

He pulled out a small, folded pack of matches; there must have been three inside at most. Suzanne was surprised, until she saw the logo on the front – it was from

1.2: The Boat

their resort. She smiled to herself, knowing he'd taken them with the intention of returning them later. Those matches had been on a journey, and only she and Dale knew the context. She can't say she fully understood the thrill of it, but in that moment, she got a taste, at least.

Dale got up onto his knees and reached out his hand.

"Thanks," Heather replied.

She leant forward and stretched out to meet him. As she took the matches, the tips of her fingers brushed the palm of his hand, just ever so slightly. As their skin touched, everything went dark – pitch black in an instant, like a light bulb suddenly blowing out.

?.?: The ???

An obnoxious repeating *bleep* disturbed the darkness.

It woke Heather instantly, as it always did. She leant over and clicked the button on top of the alarm clock. The room was darker than she expected. As she stared at the clock, her eyes started to adjust, and the glowing red lights began to form shapes: *18/11/2025 07:30 zzz* – the triple-z icon told her that she'd hit the snooze button, something she knew there wasn't time for. She fumbled with the buttons until the icon disappeared, then turned to the man snoring next to her.

"Wake up, Dale," she said, pushing her husband's shoulder with her hand. Even after thirty-five years together, it still amazed her that he could sleep through any noise.

"Come on... It's Sunday, there's no rush. They're not coming for hours," Dale grumbled sleepily.

"We've got a lot to do. Get up!"

Dale slowly rose from the bed. His fifty-two-year-old body had developed a stiffness in the joints, but he'd learnt to audibly groan through the pain. He shuffled to the ensuite to use the toilet, glancing at his face in the mirror as he did. The bags around his wrinkled eyes, his short but somehow still messy hair, his two-day stubble – all of it made him appear older than he actually was.

"What time's Lynn coming?" Dale shouted through the door, mid-stream.

?.?: The ???

"Her flight's due at ten, so she should be here around midday. I've told Aiden to be here by eleven, at the latest."

"So that means he'll be here about one then," Dale joked while washing his hands. "Is he bringing Jane?"

"She's gotta work," Heather replied, trying her best to keep her voice neutral. She was sifting through the wardrobe for something to wear.

"Thank God for that!"

"Hey, be nice about her, okay? I don't want to upset Aiden today."

"Don't worry, I'll be good." His tone was unconvincing.

The two were quietly excited for the day. Getting the whole family together in the same room had become a rare occasion, especially since Lynn had moved abroad. Aiden still lived in New Oxford, but it wasn't always possible for him to be there when Lynn visited. Both had built their own lives, which was an enormous comfort to Dale and Heather – knowing they were doing okay made them feel like they'd succeeded in their core job as parents. Still, this was the first time in almost eight months that both their kids would be home at the same time.

Dale rushed back into the bedroom as he heard his phone vibrating its way across the bedside table.

"Hey!" Heather snapped. "No work today, you promised. People don't need mortgage advice on a bloody Sunday."

"It's just Anna. She said she hopes we have a nice day, and don't forget to ask Aiden for her cake tin back."

"Did he even use it in the end?"

?.?: The ???

"Sort of…" Dale dropped his phone back on the table before smiling at his wife. "He bought Jane a cake from the supermarket, hid the box, scraped off all the frosting and decoration, then put it in the tin so it looked like he'd made it."

Heather matched his smile. "I can't decide if that's genius or really stupid."

"I think that pretty much sums up Aiden."

The two laughed together as they got ready for the day.

Dale ran the vacuum around the house, dusted every surface and wiped down the bathroom, all while Heather focused on preparing enough roast dinner to feed a small army. Or perhaps, judging by the growing mountain of peeled potatoes simmering in the pan, quite a large army. Just as she was checking on the chicken, a sudden thought brought a wave of intense panic. She pushed the bird back into the oven and ran to the stairs.

"Hun!" she shouted, trying to beat the sound of the hoover. "DAAAALE!"

"YEAH?" her husband shouted down.

"Aiden's not a vegetarian again, is he?"

"Ummm… I don't know… I think they're trying to be veggie for most of the week, but I don't think it's a complete *no* to meat. I think…"

"Okay… shit, I'll do a nut roast too just in case." Heather hastily returned to the kitchen.

?.?: The ???

They spent the morning rushing around the house, getting everything ready for the visit. To their surprise, Aiden arrived shortly after eleven. Was it Jane, his girlfriend, who was secretly the late one all this time? They both doubted that was the case.

"Hey Mum, Dad," he said as he walked into the kitchen to find them both now preparing the food. Aiden was their oldest child, only a few months from turning thirty. He had dark curly hair like his mother (though admittedly, hers was dyed now) but sadly he'd inherited his father's sense of style – evidenced by the tired jeans he wore. He'd made an effort with the simple black shirt, though, which they both took as a sign that he was looking forward to the day as much as they were.

"Hey sweetie," Heather said, leaning in to hug her son.

After returning his mum's embrace, Aiden reached out and shook his father's hand. Dale had never been much of a hugger.

"Hey Dad."

"Aiden, how's the job going?"

"Yeah, alright... boring. Anything I can do to help?"

"You could set the table?" Dale replied.

"Sure."

Lynn arrived about an hour later. Before entering her old family home, she took a moment on the porch to turn her phone off completely. It was rare that it wasn't glued to her face; her job was demanding, but she valued the time with her family too much to let it get in the way. She felt groggy from the flight, like she could just lie on the pathway right there and sleep, but you wouldn't know it to look at her. She was always impeccably dressed, something her job required that'd spilled over into her private life. Her brunette hair fell just past her ears, enough to cover her hearing aid and the temples of her wire-framed glasses. Once the phone was off, she took a long, deep breath of the bitter New Oxford morning air, then proceeded through the door.

"I'm here!" their twenty-seven-year-old daughter shouted as she dragged her suitcase through the hallway.

Hugs were exchanged, a lot of smiles, a few overlapping attempts at conversation. After a short while, the family sat around the dinner table to tackle the feast Heather and Dale (well, mostly Heather) had prepared. Bums touched seats and plates piled up as everyone started digging in – everyone except Dale. He took a moment to watch the others. It was a controlled but chaotic burst of passing vegetables, sharing gravy, and searching through the mountain of potatoes to find the crispiest ones. He gently kicked his wife under the table, attempting to distract her from her carefully calculated sprout-grabbing: *what's the minimum she could take that would allow her to say she technically had some?* The kids had once laughed at her for always cooking them with a roast when nobody ate them. She said she liked them, just to make a point, but deep down she loathed them as much as the others. Still, she couldn't lose face now, after all these years. Dale's kick was harder the second time, enough to get her attention. He nodded towards the kids, both smiling, joking about how much they were going to eat, getting on like they did when they were little. Dale and Heather were filled with an overwhelming sense of joy to have all the family together again.

"How's the job?" Dale asked his daughter, as he began taking some food from what was left (which was enough for several families).

There was no 'how are you?' or 'is life okay?' – just straight in with the work question. Lynn was used to that from her father. It wasn't that the job was more important than those things, it was just the only way he knew how to connect. To an outsider, Dale's interactions might've seemed cold, but it wasn't that – by asking anything at all he was showing interest, and there was a warmth to that.

"It's going well," Lynn said. There was a slight hesitancy before she continued, "They're opening an office in Germany. They've asked if I'd like to transfer there."

"Are you going to?" Heather asked abruptly.

"I'm not sure yet. They want me to run it, so it'd be a bit more money, a lot more responsibility, and I'd be closer to home. Germany is, what, an hour or two flight?"

"But..." Heather said in anticipation.

"But it means uprooting my whole life... again."

"Well, let us know what you decide," Dale tried not to make it too obvious that he really wanted her to take it. He knew Heather wanted that too.

"Anyway," Lynn said, changing the subject before her parents could push, "where's Jane? I was hoping to see her." She wasn't. She didn't really click with Aiden's girlfriend, but she knew how much she meant to him.

"She's working. She tried to get out of it, but they're really under pressure. Plus, she's trying to get in their good books as next year she wants to take a bunch of time off."

"Oh?" Heather said, as she poured more gravy over her modest dinner (modest in comparison to the others, anyway).

"All going well," Aiden said, smiling, excited to tell them what was on his mind, "we're planning to start trying for a baby towards the end of the year."

There was a simultaneous crash around the room as Dale and Heather both dropped their cutlery. Not for the first time that day, Heather had to hold back a tear.

"Oh Aiden," his mother said, "that's wonderful news."

"Wow, now that is exciting," Dale added, a smile across his face his son had seldom seen.

"It's early yet and nothing might happen, but it feels like the right time."

"Does that mean she's finally gonna let you sleep with her?" Lynn joked.

"Don't be crass, Lynn!" Heather interrupted, before Aiden could reply.

"What about you, Lynn?" Dale asked. "Is there someone special in your life?"

Lynn scoffed and shook her head in disappointment. "For fuck's sake, Dad."

"What?" Dale's smile slipped.

?.?: The ???

"I own my own home, have a bustling career, a full life. Yet because I don't have a partner, I'm still not seen as successful as the golden boy."

"Hey!" Heather interrupted once again. "We just want you to be happy."

"What's happiness got to do with a partner?"

"What she's saying" – Aiden's mouth lifted into a cheeky smirk – "is nobody wants her."

"Fuck you, Aiden. How you found someone to put up with your lazy arse I'll never know."

"STOP!" Dale and Heather shouted in unison. They'd seen this before: a bit of light ribbing would quickly descend into a fully-fledged family argument.

"Please, not today," Dale said.

A deadly silence fell across the room. Only the clinking of cutlery was heard as they resumed eating, the jarring sound only adding to the awkwardness lingering in the air. Dale decided to be the one to break it.

"You didn't answer me, Lynn. Is there someone special at the moment, then?" He looked his daughter in the eye, making sure she knew he was joking.

"Oh get lost!" she said playfully. She grabbed a roast potato (not a crispy one, of course – they were not to be wasted) and threw it at her father's head.

He caught it with one hand and stuffed it into his mouth. "Thramks," he mumbled.

For the rest of the meal, they talked, they ate, they laughed, they ate, they complained about eating too much, they ate. The more time they all spent together at home, the more they all regressed into how they used to be when the kids were young. It was a state of being they each found comfort in, a type of relaxation they were unable to find elsewhere in life.

Once dinner was done, Aiden cleared the table while Lynn washed the dishes. It was a chore neither minded, as it gave the siblings a chance to catch up one to one, something they both appreciated. Afterwards, the family relaxed in the living room, eating chocolate and watching *Apocalypse Cancelled*. The movie was almost as old as Aiden, but for some reason he loved it as a kid. Maybe because it was the first 15-rated movie he ever saw (at a time when he was probably too young to really understand it) and feeling like he was consuming some entertainment beyond his age was part of the appeal. Did he actually like the movie? Or did he just like the memory of the first time he was allowed to stay up late and watch a film that wasn't animated? Either way, he used to have it on repeat, much to the annoyance of his sister. Now, all these years later, the film had become a nostalgic joy for the family, something they found as comforting as the sofas they were slouched into.

    At some point during the movie's second act, when the pacing took a nosedive as they tried to pad out the runtime, Heather excused herself for a few moments. She snuck out of the back door and, once she was sure the kids couldn't see her, sparked up a cigarette. Less than a couple of minutes later, she heard a familiar voice behind her.

?.?: The ???

"Are you smoking again?" Lynn asked disapprovingly, stepping out of the house to join her. "I thought you were on patches?"

"I was. They didn't work."

"How long did you *actually* try them for? You have to give these things time to get into your system, Mum. They won't work straight away."

Heather rolled her eyes; this was exactly why she'd wanted to avoid them seeing her. It's not that she minded them knowing she smoked, she just couldn't face the lecture.

Lynn opted not to push it further. She was only there for a couple of days, and she wanted to avoid arguments. Her mother's silence confirmed that was the only way the conversation would go.

"How's the book going?" Lynn asked, attempting to change the subject.

"It's not clicking. I think I need to try something else, but I just haven't had the time. Work has been so busy."

"You've been saying that forever."

Lynn was right; Heather had always wanted to write but struggled to stick to it. Her hectic job provided a convenient excuse for not finishing anything.

"Did you just come out here to give me shit?" Heather said sharply.

"No…" Something else was clearly on Lynn's mind. "Did you tell Dad? About what happened with the car?"

"Of course not. You know he'd freak out."

?.?: The ???

The incident they were referring to was minor; somebody had driven into Lynn's car while she was waiting at a stop sign. Nobody was hurt, and both cars were able to be repaired. But they both knew that Dale wouldn't see it that way. He found the idea of his kids out on the road very unnerving after what'd happened to his brother.

As the evening drew darker, Aiden returned home in time for Jane finishing work. Lynn stayed in her old bedroom, now void of all her belongings and teenage identity, repainted and repurposed as a guest room. Still, it brought back so many memories for her.

Once Lynn was settled, and Aiden had called briefly to say he was home safe, Dale and Suzanne retreated to their bedroom.

"I'm worried about him. I'm worried he's just doing what *she* wants because it saves him from having to make a decision about his own life," Dale said, as he got changed into pyjamas.

"Maybe try talking to him on your own. He might respond to that?" Heather was in the bathroom, wiping her face with a cloth.

"I don't know, he's not one to really open up."

Heather peered around the doorway to look at her husband.

"I wonder where he gets that from."

"Yeah, yeah, I know…"

?.?: The ???

Heather left the bathroom and turned off both lights. She climbed into bed and wrapped herself around her husband.

"He'll be fine. I'm more worried about how he'll cope with a baby!"

"He'll work it out," Dale said. "We had to."

"Yeah, and I remember what that was like. It took you six months to stop holding him like a sack of potatoes."

Dale smiled, knowing it was true. "At least we knew what we were doing by the time Lynn came along."

"Speaking of," Heather said, "Germany? Think she'll go for it?"

"You know Lynn. If we seem too keen, it'll put her off. But I hope so."

"Me too." Heather tugged the cover up to her chin. "Good night, hun. Always in all ways."

Dale kissed her forehead, then held his wife tightly. Both were physically and emotionally exhausted from the day. Heather fell asleep first, as she always did. Dale stared at the ceiling for a while, feeling the warmth of his wife along his side, reflecting on how lucky he was to have such a wonderful family. It wasn't perfect, not that any family is, but it was through the imperfections that the uniqueness shined. A uniqueness that Dale, Heather, Lynn, and Aiden loved in ways they were unable to express, ways that were far too big to be captured by mere words.

Eventually, his eyes closed too. And everything turned black once again.

1.3: The Aftermath

A blinding flash caused both Dale and Heather to pull back their hands, their eyes stinging as they re-adjusted to the bright sunlight. As life came into focus, Dale realised he was on his knees, a twenty-four-year-old Heather sitting in front of him, but neither of them was sure why. He quickly surveyed his surroundings – to his right Suzanne wore a puzzled expression, while to his left there was nothing but ocean. Suddenly, he realised where he was.

He was back in Greece. Back on the boat. Back with Suzanne. Back in 1995.

Heather scurried backwards, pushing herself as far as she could into the side of the boat, her eyes filled with terror.

"You alright, babe?" Lyndon asked, trying to work out why she'd jolted. "Did you get a static shock from him or something?"

Heather didn't answer. Her heart was thumping so hard it felt like it might explode out of her chest, her breathing so fast she could barely catch it. Dale's eyes shifted in their sockets, as if trying to make some sort of sense of what had happened. As his other senses returned, he felt something in his hand, and looked down to see the book of matches. He remembered – Lyndon, Heather's boyfriend, had pushed her overboard and she'd lost her lighter. Dale had matches, and was passing them to Heather when their hands touched, and then suddenly there was… Something? Nothing? Darkness? Light?

1.3: The Aftermath

"Dale, what's wrong?" Suzanne asked, leaning in front of him to catch his attention.

When that failed, she grabbed his head with both hands in an attempt to steady him. Dale's eyes drifted to Suzanne but he was unable to speak; he had more to say than he could process. It was like there were too many words in his throat, and he didn't know in what order to release them. Instead, he just panted heavily.

"Heather... HEATHER!" Lyndon held his girlfriend's shoulders and tried to shake her out of her stupor.

The other couples on the deck began to shift, reacting to the confusion around them.

Heather snapped to life. She turned to face Dale and noticed him staring back at her.

"Hun," she whispered, her voice filled with a confused vulnerability.

The two of them pushed past their partners and hugged in the middle of the deck. They held one another tightly, Dale physically shaking, tears streaming down Heather's face. Their embrace was quickly disrupted as Lyndon pushed his hand between them with force, pulling them apart.

"What the fuck!?" he shouted, his face reddening angrily.

"What's going on?" Moira, the wife of the older couple, asked from the corner. She got up onto her knees, ready to spring into action if things got more serious.

1.3: The Aftermath

Despite being pulled apart, Heather and Dale's gaze remained locked, both hoping to find answers in the eyes of the other – and both failing to do so.

Lyndon waved his hand in front of his girlfriend, trying to break her stare. "Heather, what the fuck? Who is this?"

It worked. As Heather snapped out of it, Dale turned back to Suzanne, noticing her face twisted in concern.

"Dale, do you know her?"

Finally, from somewhere, Dale found the strength to speak. "This... this is Heather Sawyer,"

"Like you, Sawyer? Is she your cousin or something?" Suzanne asked.

"Sawyer? Her name isn't Sawyer!" Lyndon snapped, a growing irritation in his voice. "It's Heather Wiley!"

"She's my wife," Dale said, his tone factual.

The entire top deck fell silent as the nonsensical words sat heavy in the air.

"You're married? What the hell?" Suzanne yelled.

Lyndon sprung to his feet. "She's not your wife! Heather, who is this clown?"

Heather shook her head, not in a way that suggested Dale was wrong, but as if trying to clear her thoughts. Without saying a word, she hurried to her feet, then climbed down the ladder.

"We need to get off this boat," she shouted as she descended.

1.3: The Aftermath

Heather begged the staff to turn the boat around and head back to shore. They laughed at the absurdity of the idea at first, but once they saw the anguish in her face, they had no choice but to agree. They offered to call a doctor to meet her at the dock, but she refused – she just wanted to get home. Realising they might want to be alone, the staff took her and Lyndon down to the tiny kitchen below deck, where the two of them stayed for the remainder of the journey. Heather, much like Dale was doing on the top deck, attempted to articulate her impossible thoughts to her partner. They hadn't had a moment to process what had happened for themselves – how could they possibly explain it to somebody else?

Once the boat hit shore, both couples rushed off as quickly as they could, ignoring the glares as they weaved hurriedly through inconvenienced passengers. Few words were exchanged between the four of them, but they agreed to head to the nearest (and quietest) place that served coffee. They found somewhere not far from the dock, a small cafe with a name written with few recognisable letters, not that any of them took more than a glance at it. The outdoor seating was packed, but luckily because of the intense heat, indoors was empty. This was exactly what they needed – a quiet place to talk.

Dale took a seat first, his head pounding, like the day had inflated his brain to the point where it was far too big for his skull. Heather instinctively sat next to him, grabbed his hand, and started rubbing it with her fingers to calm him. It usually did the trick. Or... it *will* usually do the trick?

1.3: The Aftermath

She noticed Lyndon and Suzanne staring at her in disbelief. She let go of Dale's hand and hastily shuffled to the opposite end of the table. A frustrated Lyndon took a seat next to her, with Suzanne opposite, her arms folded, clearly uncomfortable. The staff brought over a couple of large freestanding fans. They did little to help with the heat, but they appreciated them all the same. After serving them coffee, the staff left the group to it. The humid air had somehow thickened since they'd walked in, and it was clear they needed some time alone.

"So… you swear you two didn't know each other before the boat?" Lyndon asked.

"I swear," Heather insisted.

"And then you touched," he continued. "When this guy passed you the matches, you both touched, and then you flew back like you'd seen a ghost. But what you're saying is, in that fraction of a second, you both disappeared for thirty-five years?"

"It was a day," Dale replied.

Lyndon glared at him, grimacing. Heather rested her hand on his arm in an attempt to reassure him that she was there. She could feel the tension in his muscles.

"To us," she said calmly, "it just felt like we'd been gone for one day. But it was a day in the future, and Dale and I had been together for over thirty-five years."

"That doesn't make sense," Suzanne said, scrunching her eyes.

Heather continued, "I know. None of this makes sense. I can't explain it, I can only tell you what happened. We

1.3: The Aftermath

experienced one day, but we had the memories of a whole life together."

"So you think you saw the future?" Lyndon shouted. "You two meet here, in Greece, on that boat. And then, what? You spend the next thirty-five years together?"

"That's the other thing that doesn't make sense." Heather stared into her thick black coffee, as if trying to find the answers hidden in the dark abyss. "The day we shared wasn't thirty-five years in the future, it was less than that. I don't get it." She turned her attention to a silent Dale, who was staring off away from the group. "The maths doesn't work. Dale, we were already together by now, right? In whatever we saw, we met a few years ago, at your brother's funeral."

"Jak's not dead," Suzanne said abruptly.

"What?" Heather reached across the table and touched her husband... her ex-husband... her future husband? "Dale?"

He turned his attention to the others, his face a mess with calculation.

"It wasn't the future," he said, his voice quiet, whispery. "At least, it wasn't *this* future."

While the others had been talking, Dale had taken a moment to reflect and put his thoughts in order, trying to make sense of the day. Each conclusion he found only invited more questions. It wasn't like pulling a thread – it was like pulling *all* the threads at once, and watching them tangle the more he tugged. But there was *one* thing he'd noticed.

1.3: The Aftermath

He downed his bitter coffee before telling the others his realisation.

"When I was seventeen, Jak, my brother, was in a car accident. He was going over a roundabout when some overconfident boy racer pulled out in front of him. They hit, and the car behind Jak slammed into them both. They said Jak's car bonnet folded like it was made of paper. When it snapped, it came through his windscreen and impaled him right through his chest. He was paralysed from the waist down. The doctors called his survival a miracle… 1 mm, they said. 1 mm more to the left and he would have died. That's how close he was to the end."

"Shit," Heather said. "In our life... in our *other* life, the vision, Jak died in that crash. It was after his funeral that you came into the Red Lion where I worked. That's where we met."

"Exactly," Dale said. "He didn't die here, so you and I never met."

Without saying a word, Suzanne left the table and rushed for the door. Within a second, she was outside, and in another she was gone from sight. Dale froze solid, unsure of what to do.

"You should go after her, hun," Heather said delicately, reaching across the table once again to touch him, instinctually wanting to offer him comfort however she could.

Dale listened to the instruction, not necessarily because he agreed, but because he had too much information to process and was grateful for somebody telling him what to

1.3: The Aftermath

do. He walked past the physically shaking Lyndon and ran for the door.

"Suzanne!" Dale shouted as he left the cafe. The nosy eyes of the outdoor diners watched as he tried to catch up with her. She only sped up as she heard his approach.

"Suzanne, please just let me explain!" he shouted again, trying his best to ignore the stares.

His steps quickened into a stride, then a jog, but it took almost a sprint to catch her up. He grabbed her arm to slow her, but she pulled it away from him.

"What the fuck, Dale?"

"Just wait a second, would you?!"

They both stopped, taking a few seconds to catch their breath. She turned to reveal a face he'd not seen before. It was a mixture of pain, anger, and loss.

"This is messed up," she screamed, her hands flailing in the air. "What the hell is this?"

"I don't know…" Dale was still trying to breathe.

"Is this some, what, sick elaborate prank? Some way to break up with me? Did you and her set this up?"

"I don't know what this is!" Dale shouted. It was the first time Suzanne had heard him raise his voice – she hadn't thought he was capable of doing so, he was always so level. "I don't know, alright? I don't know what's going on any more than you do. One minute we were on that boat, the next we were somewhere else."

1.3: The Aftermath

"Why didn't we just do the quad bikes?" Suzanne sighed. She was calmer than before, the agitation still clear but softened a little around the edges.

"I don't know, but we didn't. For some reason I got on that boat today, and for some reason I saw what I saw. *We* saw what we saw. I can't change that now."

Suzanne raised her eyes to meet Dale's and couldn't help but ask the question burning in the back of her mind, knowing, deep down, she wouldn't want to hear the answer.

"Do you love her?"

Dale didn't even hesitate. "Of course I love her. She's my wife. She's the mother of my children."

Suzanne scoffed and walked away again.

This time, Dale didn't follow.

1.4: The Evening

As night fell on Corfu, the temperature dropped just enough to make being outside *almost* bearable. Almost. The air was as humid as it had been during the day, maybe more so, but the intensity had slightly dialed down. This was something Dale was grateful for. He was waiting alone for Heather to join him outside the block of apartments where she was staying, but it had been an hour and there was still no sign.

It didn't worry him though – he knew she'd show. He knew everything about her. Only twenty-four hours ago she'd been a total stranger, but now he knew her better than anyone else in the world. It wasn't like her to be late; Dale's lack of punctuality often wound her up, because Heather was only ever late with good reason.

Anyway, he didn't mind waiting. Without the noise of the day, he was left only with the gentle sounds of the ocean waves and the quiet hum of distant traffic. Whenever he had an *unusual* day, Dale would take some time to find somewhere peaceful and put his thoughts together – and this had been the most unusual of days. But how do you organise two sets of memories? It wasn't like they were competing for dominance, it was just as if both sets existed simultaneously – like two different pieces of music playing in both ears at the same time, faintly, but always there. He believed if he focused on them, he'd be able to find a collective rhythm, the first step in making sense of it all. But whenever he tried, both melodies just grew louder.

1.4: The Evening

The disjointed symphony was disrupted as Heather came bounding through the door behind him, her face hot with stress from whatever had happened inside.

"Hey hun," she said, taking a moment to recentre herself. She took a long, deep breath, followed by an even deeper sigh.

"Hey…"

Dale awkwardly extended his arms for a hug, swapped that for an attempted kiss, then presented his hand for a shake. "What do we do here?" he asked, puzzled. "Do we hug? Are we formal?"

Heather nodded and her eyes shifted upwards, as if signalling Dale to look. He glanced up to see Lyndon, several floors above, staring at them through the window.

"I know what I'm going to do." Heather reached into the pocket of her bright flowing trousers and pulled out a packet of cigarettes. She took one out, then angled the pack towards Dale.

"Have you already given up by now? I can't remember when you did."

"Give up?" Dale shook his head. "I never started here." He playfully knocked her with his elbow. "I guess I only started because I met you."

Heather smiled and lit her cigarette, using one of the many spare lighters she had in the apartment. A thought occurred to her – if she'd taken one of the spares with her on the boat, none of this would have happened. Dale had seen Heather smoke almost every day they were together,

1.4: The Evening

and yet the first drag that night was the longest he'd ever seen her take.

"Where's Suzanne?" she asked, smoke flowing smoothly from her mouth in all directions.

"She's..." Dale kicked his feet. "She's gone to the airport."

"Oh, I'm sorry. What did she make of it all?"

"She thought it was some practical joke that we were taking too far. I don't know. I don't blame her for leaving. We'd only been together a few months... I'd have done the same."

Heather looked back up towards the apartment, aware that Lyndon was still watching like a hawk.

"Can we get out of here?"

"Sure."

The two began to walk slowly away from the apartments. There was no particular direction, they were just moving for the sake of moving, wandering aimlessly side by side.

Dale looked back at the apartments to see the curtains close, Lyndon disappearing into the depths of the room.

"What about him? How's he coping?" Dale knew what the answer was likely to be.

"He doesn't know what to think. He's known me long enough to understand I'm not making it up. But he's confused, worried, scared."

"What about you, Heather?"

1.4: The Evening

"I'm confused too… and worried… and scared. I mean, how do we get past this? What are we meant to do?"

"I don't know." Dale shrugged. "I'm sorry, Heather. That this happened, I mean."

"I'm not." She looked towards him and smiled, glad that she hadn't taken a spare lighter with her on the boat. "Don't get me wrong, Dale, this is a mess. I have no idea what happened, or why it happened, or how it happened… but I wouldn't want to go back to not knowing you now."

"Yeah, I know what you mean."

He fought the urge to wrap his arms around her. He fought the urge to grab her right there and then, tell her to just run away with him, to go and recreate the life they saw. But he knew it wasn't as simple as that.

"Dale… We're flying home in the morning. Lyndon just wants us back to the comfort of our own space. He cried… I didn't even know he was capable of crying. I know there's a lot to work out, between me and you, but I must think of him too and what he needs."

"Yeah, I get it." Dale swallowed what he really wanted to say. This situation was delicate, complicated and painful. It needed time.

"What will you do, hun? You can't stay here on your own, especially without sunscreen," she joked, playfully returning the elbow bump.

"What makes you think I don't have any?"

"Come on, Dale, you always forget."

1.4: The Evening

"Well, maybe in this... whatever it is, I don't forget as much."

"Let me guess," she said, rolling her eyes. "Your forgetfulness was my fault too."

"Maybe... but as it happens I did actually forget. I've been using Suzanne's."

"Ha! I knew it."

The two found themselves on the beach, slowly shuffling across the sliver of sand that hadn't been consumed by the night sea. They both stared out into the distance as they moved, not at anything in particular, just watching. They'd sense others occasionally pass them by, but neither acknowledged it. They were focused on the walk, the sand, the sea, the sky, but, mostly, each other. Suddenly, they heard a joyful scream from a nearby resort. They looked on to see a German couple attempting to dance on the tables – they'd clearly been enjoying the all-inclusive bar. Dale smiled gleefully as an old memory came to the surface.

"Do you remember our holiday in Turkey?"

Heather joined him in quiet laughter. "I knew you were going to bring that up!"

"You were so wasted. Anna had to physically restrain you from running into the ocean. You were determined you wanted to swim, even though you could barely walk!"

"I can't remember much of that night."

"I'm not surprised," Dale chuckled. "You were always such a joyful drunk." His smile became deeper, more

1.4: The Evening

reflective. "It's weird seeing you like this. So young, I mean. You look like you did back when we first met."

"I know what you mean. When I caught myself in the mirror earlier, it surprised me, too."

"What about me?" Dale asked. "Do I look younger?"

Heather took a moment to examine the details of his face — his faded green eyes that looked almost grey in moonlight, his chapped lips that would tear as soon as the weather got cold, his ruffled hair that some would call messy, but she appreciated the distinct Dale-style. Or, rather, lack of. It was a face that held so many wonderful memories for her.

"Nah," she joked. "You've always looked the same."

"Thanks, I'll take that as a compliment... I think."

Heather pulled the cigarettes from her pocket and lit another one. It was her fifth in a row — she'd barely stubbed one out before lighting the next.

"Have you spoken to Anna yet? About today, I mean?"

"Not yet. I keep going to WhatsApp her, then I remember I'm about a decade or so too early for that."

"There is something nice about not being able to be glued to my phone," Heather said. "Without Twitter, I now know that there are exactly three hundred and twenty-seven tiles in the bathroom of our apartment here."

There was a moment of silence as the two reflected on the things they no longer had. The air between them grew unnaturally cold, their smiles slipping, as they both thought about something they'd been avoiding.

1.4: The Evening

"Have you..." Dale started, working hard to get through it, "you know... thought about *them*?"

Heather wrapped the bottom of her shirt around her finger and used it to wipe a tear from her eye.

"Dale, I... I can't think about them."

"I know. I can't yet either. It feels impossible."

"I feel like they're away somewhere, on a different holiday in some other part of the world... And when we get home, we'll see them again. But deep down I know that's not it, and soon I'm going to have my heart shatter in ways I can't imagine. But right now... I don't have the capacity to face that, you know?"

"I do. I wish I didn't, but I do."

The silence returned. They slowly wandered back towards the apartments. It wasn't that they had nothing to say – on the contrary, it was that they had *too much* to say. Their suitcase was packed to the point of bursting, and if they undid the clip, even just a little, it would explode out like a volcano and cover everything. Repacking it would take far longer than one evening. They doubted it would ever fit back in there.

Eventually, they found themselves back at Heather's apartment block. Walking together had been nice.

No, more than nice.

Being together, just the two of them, doing much of nothing together...

It had been home.

1.4: The Evening

As their walk came to an end, they looked at each other and smirked.

"I love you, Dale," Heather said softly. It was something he'd heard a million times before, yet he never tired of it. It felt as impactful now as the day she first said it. "I don't know what will happen, but I do know I'll always love you. Always in all ways."

"Always in all ways, Heather."

The two smiled together. It was sweet, friendly, loving, but tainted with a sadness and uncertainty that they could both see in the other's eyes.

"What do we do now?" she whispered, barely louder than the wind.

"What *can* we do? You need to head home with Lyndon. I'll see if I can get a flight back tomorrow too, or the next day. We know where each other lives, right? We just take this one day at a time."

"One day at a time…"

The two took a final moment to look at each other. Their backgrounds faded as they stared, both plucking up the courage to face the reality of the situation. They had no idea what to say, no idea what to do, no idea what the future held. All they knew was that nothing would ever be the same again.

Part 2
The Birthday
1 year after the vision

2.1: The Walk

It was a bitter Saturday evening in New Oxford, not that the cold had stopped anyone from heading out. The streets were alive with strobe lights, thumping music, and drunk dancers, all overflowing from the various pubs and clubs that littered the centre. This was fairly typical for the city and was why Dale and Anna usually avoided the area over the weekends. This particular weekend, however, was different.

Their destination was on the opposite side of the city, and the two friends had no choice but to cross through the centre. *Walk* may not be the right word for what Dale was doing – he was a few steps short of a sprint.

"Slow down!" Anna said, straggling a few paces behind. She wasn't used to walking so fast in her boots. She wasn't used to wearing a dress, either.

"Sorry!" Dale slowed enough for Anna to catch up. "We're just running a little late."

"And whose fault is that, exactly?" she scoffed.

"Yeah, yeah, I know…"

Anna wasn't used to Dale moving so fast for anything. She definitely wasn't used to seeing him in an ironed shirt and trousers. She could tell from the excessive layers of aftershave that he was making an effort. *More than he should*, she thought.

"You're not going to just abandon me all night, are you?" she asked, hoping for reassurance.

2.1: The Walk

Even though Dale had slowed, he was still several steps ahead of Anna, as if trying to usher her along.

"Why would I?"

"Just, don't..." she said. "Remember, I'm your guest."

"You mean like how you abandoned me at Sanja's eighteenth?" he jested.

"That was different. I was sick!"

"Yeah, sick of being around Sanja's weird brother banging on about his airsoft guns."

Anna laughed. "I forgot all about him!"

"I didn't. That guy is burnt into my mind forever... *These are what they use to train real soldiers*," Dale said in a mock tone.

"I can't believe he thought that would impress Jess!"

The pathways darkened as they left the city centre and entered one of the many surrounding residential areas. Dale looked at his watch – they were already late. But wasn't it cool to be late to a party? He'd heard people say that before. He noticed that he'd stormed too far ahead again and stopped to let his friend catch up. This time, he walked by her side, wanting to make sure she was okay.

"Are you actually worried about tonight?"

"Not worried. I just don't know anyone there... Don't go leaving me with a bunch of randos."

"You know Heather. She's not a rando."

Anna rolled her eyes, as she had done many times in the last few months.

2.1: The Walk

"I've met her like, twice, I think? And it's always weird and awkward how she talks to me. It's as if she's known me my whole life."

"She did know you for a whole life."

"Yeah, that's weird too. Don't do that."

Anna didn't really understand what Dale had gone through, but she had tried her best to sympathise. That was challenging whenever the conversation involved *the other Anna*. It was something she found uncomfortable to discuss.

Dale looked at his friend and realised her concern was genuine. "I won't leave you alone, I promise."

"Good," she said, "because if I wanted to spend all night trying to liven up a conversation, I'd have stayed home with Bob."

Dale smiled, one reserved just for Anna. "How is my favourite accountant? I've not seen him for a while."

"He's..." She paused a beat. She'd always been able to tell Dale anything – it was one of the things she loved about their friendship. But still, sometimes it took some building up before she could put the words into the world and make them real. "Something is going on, something he's not talking about. Sometimes I wake up in the middle of the night, and I notice he's still awake. He says he's been sleeping, but I don't think he has. I think he's more stressed than he's letting on, I think he's trying not to put it on me with everything I've got going on at the moment. But I wish he would. He's been like it since his uncle made contact again. He said in that Bob way that 'everything is fine', but I think it's shaken him. I just don't know how—"

2.1: The Walk

Dale interrupted her, failing to hear the vulnerability in her voice. "I'm sure it'll be fine, probably just some work stuff. You know Bob, he's always fine. Ha, in a way I've known Bob longer you have."

"Don't do that," Anna said with a crumpled frown. "That's gross. I asked you before not to talk about us in your… whatever happened."

Dale laughed it off, and Anna swallowed what she was trying to say. Dale was too focused on getting to the party and it was obvious he wasn't going to listen. She huffed and gently shook her head, mostly to herself, but a part of her was hoping he'd notice.

He didn't.

"I know what you mean though. I spoke to Heather a couple of days ago. I could tell there were things she wanted to say, but she just couldn't."

"That's really not the same at all, Dale."

Anna realised the conversation was about to become Heather-centric again, as so many of their conversations had recently. She thought about her parents, watching how small sparks of tension would blow up like bombs by the end of the day. It was like a rubber band – the longer things went unsaid, the more it stretched, and eventually it would snap. The difference here was that Dale didn't even know it was stretching.

"Dale," she said, with a more serious look across her face than he was used to, "I was trying to talk to you then about some concerns I have. You're the only person I can talk to about this stuff. You know what I've been through,

2.1: The Walk

you know how hard it is to talk about anything in my life, but I was trusting you, and you just dismissed it."

Dale was taken aback. He was shocked, not only that he hadn't noticed what he'd done, but also that she'd been so forward in bringing it to his attention. He was grateful for the latter – he hated the idea of spending all night at the party without knowing he'd upset his best friend. He had to be more careful.

"Anna, I know since the vision happened, I've been a bit less *me*..."

"Sometimes, Dale, it's like you're only half here. Your body is here, but your mind is somewhere else."

"That's fair."

That's exactly how Dale had felt for much of the time over the last year – present in body, absent in mind.

"I'm not going to pretend to know what you went through," Anna said softly. "I can't imagine how confusing it must be. But I'm doing everything I can to be here for you through this. I need you to be here for me too."

"I will," he said. What he said next was something Anna had only heard him say maybe two or three times in the whole time they'd known each other. Not even just to her – she doubted he'd ever said it to anyone else. It was not that he didn't feel it, in fact she was sure he did, but Dale was never one to admit how he felt about anything.

"I'm sorry, you know."

2.1: The Walk

Anna put her arm around him. "Don't worry, we're good, Dale… But that might change if I have to spend the whole night feeling awkward."

"If it does get awkward and you want to break the ice tonight," Dale said, "just give Heather her present. That'll make you feel more a part of the group."

"Present?"

"Yeah…"

"I haven't got her a present." Anna let go of Dale. The two stopped in an alleyway as Anna began to freak out.

"What?" Dale remained completely straight faced.

"Why would I have a present?"

"Because it's her birthday… we're going to her party… at her house…"

"Fuck!" Anna shouted, throwing her arms up in the air. "Are you serious? I hardly know her. I didn't even think about it!"

"Are you joking? It's a birthday party, what did you expect?" he said, a mock-annoyed tone in his voice.

"Fuck, Dale! Fuuuuck!"

She watched as her friend's mouth began to wiggle, the corner lifting just enough to give him away. Finally, he broke and laughed. "I'm just winding you up!"

"You're such an idiot," Anna said, relieved. "My heart was in my throat then."

"Anyway, what I've got her is enough for both of us." He smiled proudly.

Anna winced. "Dale…" she said gently.

2.1: The Walk

"What?"

"I just... I hope you haven't got her something really expensive. Don't show up Lyndon, okay?"

"Trust me." Dale grinned. "I've barely spent a penny."

2.2: The Party

The house was filled with the sounds of Jon Bon Jovi, a lifelong – lives-long – favourite of Heather's. She'd clearly picked the music for the night. The fact she wasn't yet wailing along to *Bad Medicine* suggested she was still firmly on the safe side of sober. The music was accompanied by the enthused rumblings of old friends catching up in almost every room of the house.

The lounge was the epicentre of the celebration – a hive of conversation and laughter. The kitchen, on the other hand, was the polar opposite – picking at the snacks kept people too busy to talk. Naturally, this was where Anna and Dale gravitated to, away from the noise, and within reaching distance of the food. It wasn't that they were hungry, just that eating always helped cut through the awkwardness of being in a house full of strangers. For Anna, anyway. For Dale, a word didn't exist to capture the situation he was in.

Everywhere he looked were strangers he knew well – Heather's friends and family, people he'd spent decades getting to know, people he'd had connections with, in-jokes, banter, experiences... But all that was before. Or after. Or both? He shared a lifetime of one-sided future-history with these people. He knew them all, but none of them knew him.

Joshua, an old school friend of Heather's, was grabbing a beer from the fridge. When he and his wife were moving house, they used Dale as their mortgage advisor, and something between the two men just clicked. They became

2.2: The Party

friends for a short while, went for a couple of beers, before it eventually fizzled out... as these things do.

Through the patio doors, chatting in the garden, were Charlotte and Abby. Charlotte worked with Heather back when she was at the bar and Abby was a regular customer. Whenever there was a party, the two would stick together like magnets. For a long time, both were too shy to be honest about their feelings, but after almost a decade Abby had a few too many and told Charlotte how much she really liked her. The two got married not long after that. Dale pondered how much of their lives they were wasting trying to find the courage to speak their truths.

One voice in the lounge mounted above all others – that was Ishan, always the loudest man in the room. He was telling awful cheesy jokes, but from the explosions of laughter following each punchline, they were going down a treat. Typical Ishan – he could always read the room and knew exactly what to do and say to keep everyone entertained. Over the years, Ishan had a pretty standard life. He had a good job, a good house, a good wife. To an onlooker he seemed happy, content and peaceful... but he proved everyone wrong there. His mind was anything *but* peaceful, as the police discovered when they found him in his car outside the station, shotgun in hand, brain splattered across the windscreen. He'd chosen that location because he figured the police would be best equipped for and least disturbed by the grisly scene. They were trained for that, he reasoned – more than most, anyway.

And yet... none of that happened. Or had happened yet. And maybe now it never would? All Dale wanted to do

2.2: The Party

was go up to them and talk like old times, to join Joshua in grabbing a beer from the fridge, to tell Charlotte and Abby their feelings were reciprocated, to take Ishan away from the crowd and ask him how he was really doing. But he couldn't. As he'd discovered over the last few months, these things never played out like they did in his head, and all it did was freak people out when he tried. Heather, at least, was checking in on Ishan every chance she got. Dale could hear her in the other room, his ears trained to pick up the exact tone of her voice. God, did he miss that voice...

"Hey!" Anna clicked her fingers in his face. "You said you wouldn't leave me alone."

"I'm right here." Dale wiped his eyes, realising he'd been stuck in a daydream.

"Your mind is somewhere else again. Are you doing okay?"

"I'm fine," he said, grabbing a sausage roll from the counter. There were only a handful left – Anna and Dale had worked their way through the whole plate. "It's just... weird, you know?"

"I don't... Do you wanna go?"

"We've only just got here. I haven't even beaten you at pool yet." Dale winked.

"There's a pool table here?"

"Yeah, Heather has a table in the basement."

Anna threw her arms in the air. "Then why the fuck are we wasting time in the kitchen?"

"I thought you'd wanna be by the food."

2.2: The Party

"Well, here's an idea, Dale," she said sarcastically, as she lifted her plate from the counter. "We take the food with us."

"Oh no... Heather is *very* protective of that table. Everyone knows you can't have food in the basement."

"Well, damn." She quickly contemplated the options. "Now I'm torn."

Before Anna could decide, the two were disrupted by another couple approaching the food table. Dale didn't recognise them. Both were tall, slim, tanned, with razor-sharp cheekbones and not a single hair out of place. They looked like supermodels. They exchanged awkward smiles as they began piling a plate up with... salad? *Who goes for the salad at a party?* both Dale and Anna thought.

"I always eat too much at these things," the woman said.

Anna smiled politely and resisted the urge to tell her to fuck off when she spotted the half-handful of lettuce on the woman's plate.

"I'm Tonya, this is Sebastian," Tonya said, determined to make small talk.

"I'm Anna... this is Dale."

"How do you two know Heather?" Dale asked, trying to figure out why he didn't know them.

"I'm Lyndon's sister, this is my partner." Ah, that made sense. "What about you two?"

2.2: The Party

"Oh, I, uhh..." Dale hesitated. It was a simple question, but the answer was anything *but* simple. "We met on holiday."

The cogs turned rapidly behind Tonya's eyes.

"Dale... you're *that* Dale. With the thing."

"What thing, babe?" Sebastian asked.

"Remember? Lyndon told us that story about Heather and Dale. They saw the future or something."

"Oh yeah!" Sebastian said. "Hey, you don't know the lottery numbers, do you?"

Dale laughed politely. Inside he was screaming. "Sadly not."

"Well, we'll see you around," Tonya said, excusing herself and Sebastian. Their enthusiasm to make small talk had dissipated as soon as they realised who Dale was.

"Enjoy your fucking salad," Anna grumbled as soon as they were out of earshot. She grabbed the plate of mini pizzas and passed one to Dale.

"You're right," Dale said, "maybe we should just..." His mouth lifted to a smile before he could finish his sentence. His face began to glow as the voice he was tuned into grew louder. Heather stepped into the kitchen, wearing an elegant floral blouse over bright jeans. She smiled when she spotted Dale and Anna.

Dale's glow subsided when he noticed Lyndon put his muscled arm around his girlfriend, pulling her in a little tighter than what would be considered normal. Or what

2.2: The Party

would be considered comfortable. He always did that when Dale was around.

"You're here!" Heather said, a huge grin across her face.

"Happy birthday, Heather." Dale leant in to kiss her on the cheek.

"Hey, happy birthday," Anna said, not that anyone was listening to her. Heather and Dale had locked eyes.

"Thank you both for coming. Have you got drinks?" Heather asked, ready to grab them both one if they said no. She was always an attentive host.

"We're good."

"Alright," Lyndon said with a nod.

"Hey, Lyndon, how are you?" Dale asked.

Without replying, Lyndon pulled his girlfriend away. "Heather, I think they're shouting for you in the other room."

Heather threw Dale an apology shrug as she followed Lyndon out of the kitchen.

Heather flitting between people while she was hosting a party wasn't unusual, but Lyndon made it clear he was uncomfortable around Dale. It didn't matter how much they talked about what happened, the situation never improved. In fact, it made it worse. It was like they'd given him a book that explained the complexities of what happened and how they felt. They tried adding more words to it, but all it did was make the book heavier to carry.

2.3: The Gift

"Sometimes I sleep, sometimes it's not for dayyyys, the people I meet, always go their separate ways! Sometimes you tell me buh booooouuu drink, and times when you're alone, all you do is think. I'M A COWBOY! ON A STEEL HORSE I RIDE! AND I'M WANTED, WAAAAANNNTEEED, DEAD OR ALIVE!"

The music faded unexpectedly. The chorus of Heather-led screeching voices turned to laughter as they heard themselves bellowing unaccompanied by the music.

Attention turned to Lyndon, who, having just adjusted the volume on the sound system, was now banging a spoon on his pint glass. Guests from the other rooms began to congregate in the lounge. This included Dale and Anna, who had been busy playing a game of *guess which guest was going to moan about how little food was left next*, a game they'd inadvertently caused. The duo followed the crowd in from the kitchen and stood in the doorway watching.

Once everyone was there, Lyndon stopped banging the glass and signalled Heather to join him. She giggled as she walked over, awkwardly waving to the rest of the party.

"Now that I've got your attention," Lyndon started, "I just wanted to wish Heather, my wonderful partner, a happy birthday. You're halfway to fifty now, babe!"

Heather playfully tapped him on the leg.

2.3: The Gift

"But seriously, thank you all for coming tonight. I know it means a lot to Heather, and it does to me too. As some of you know, this has been a challenging year for us…"

There were a few subtle (though not subtle enough) side-glances over to Dale from the handful of people that knew who he was.

"But," Lyndon continued, "like all challenges, it's very easy to get consumed by it. Here now, surrounded by so many people that we love, it shows us just how lucky we are. So, I'd like to raise a toast" – Lyndon lifted his drink high into the air – "to Heather!"

"To Heather!" the crowd shouted. They knocked glasses and exchanged smiles.

"Now, there's one last thing…" Lyndon said.

Dale's heart sank into his chest. Surely he wouldn't propose on her birthday, would he? Anna grabbed his hand and squeezed it, hard. *Shit.* She obviously suspected the same.

"If you know Heather well, then you'll know that she always waits until everyone has left before she opens any presents." There were a few agreeing rumbles around the room. Lyndon continued, "And as nice as that is, babe, it means nobody gets to see your reaction!"

All the anxiety drained from Dale in an instant, like a rush of pins and needles all over. He'd got it wrong.

"Well, tonight we change that!"

"Lyndon, no," Heather said quietly.

"What do you think, guys?" he shouted over the crowd.

2.3: The Gift

The house roared with confirmation.

"Fine!" She smiled awkwardly. "Just the one!"

Heather grabbed a gift from the overflowing table. It was a small white box tied with ruby ribbon.

"To Heather," she said reading the label aloud. "Happy birthday. I saw this and it made me think of you. Love from Sally."

She waved to her friend Sally, who was beaming with excitement to see Heather open the gift.

She carefully pulled the bow, then took the top off the box to reveal a glass ornament of a horse on its hind legs.

"Oh Sally, this is beautiful!" Heather said, overjoyed with her gift.

At least, that was how it looked on the surface – but Dale knew how much she'd have hated it deep down. She despised tat, ornaments, trinkets, and she wasn't even a big fan of horses! He held back his laughter. He could tell from Lyndon's face that he'd bought the lie. That made Dale warm inside, realising that he still knew her better than her boyfriend did.

"Do you really like it?" Sally asked from across the room.

"I love it, thank you so much!" Heather replied, carefully placing the horse back into the box. A box it would likely never leave again.

Heather looked back to the gift table, temptation in her eyes. She'd enjoyed opening that more than she thought she would, even if the gift was a dud!

2.3: The Gift

"Oh... maybe one more!" she said. It became clear to everyone in the room that she was about to work through the whole table. She grabbed another one from the pile, a long, rectangular box, messily wrapped in far more plain blue paper than was needed.

Dale recognised the paper... *shit*, it was his. Before he could say anything, she was already reading the label.

"To Heather. I saw this and couldn't resist getting it for you. Happy birthday. Always in all ways. Lo... umm... *from Dale*."

Lyndon rolled his eyes, making his disapproval obvious to the whole room.

Heather tore the paper, much less gently than she had with Sally's gift, and hastily opened the box. Anna's face filled with dread. She looked at her friend as if to say, *this is already awkward enough, I hope you haven't just made it worse.* Heather reached into the box, and pulled out...

A banana?

Everyone, Heather included, stared at the gift in confusion. She held the banana up, as if presenting it to Dale. "Umm... thanks?"

"There's another one," Dale said, too quiet for her to hear.

"What?"

"On the table... the other blue one."

Heather's eyes darted back to the gifts. She sifted through a few until she spotted the smaller but equally-messily-wrapped-in-far-too-much-plain-blue-paper box. She

2.3: The Gift

put down the banana and picked up the second gift, once again making quick work of the paper. She burst into laughter the second she saw inside the box, so much so that she struggled to speak. The crowd watched as she pulled a toy car, a red Volkswagen beetle, from the box.

There was no reaction from the party. The car had clearly not helped explain the banana – if anything, it'd made it more confusing. But Heather understood.

"Right," she said, knowing she needed to provide some context to her reaction. "Let me explain. So it was, umm, when was it, Dale? Twenty years ago? And we were in Dubai, and we went to hire a car, right, and we walked up to the salesman, and we were trying to explain that…" Looking up at the blank faces of her guests, she realised that her explanation was just adding to the confusion.

In the corner of her eye, she saw Lyndon, unimpressed by what had unfolded, downing the remainder of his beer. Her face dropped, and she flicked her eyes towards Dale, looking for reassurance. He subtly shook his head, as if to tell her not to continue. *They won't understand*, he said without words.

"Twenty years ago?" a male voice shouted from the crowd. "What, when you were like, five?"

"For fuck's sake," Lyndon spat. He stormed out of the room, slamming the door as he left. The loud bang reverberated around the room, everyone standing in awkward silence. Heather froze, unsure what to say or do.

Go, Dale mouthed to her.

2.3: The Gift

Without saying a word, she cranked the volume on the music, then ran after Lyndon.

2.4: The Porch

The party was back in full swing, the music having helped lift the mood. This time, it was a mega mix of eighties dance classics. The excited sounds of the crowd were just loud enough to fight over the melodic sounds of *Take On Me*. As midnight came and went, the music continued to get louder. At first, it was to detract from the ongoing argument happening upstairs. By the time the shouting had subsided, the guests had forgotten all about what'd happened with the gifts.

Heather, however, was alone on the porch outside the front door. She was taking a few minutes to recentre before attempting to re-join the celebrations. She was glad she'd warned the neighbours about the party, many of whom had now wandered over to join in. She sat still, only moving to occasionally sip her evening tea. She couldn't be happier that her friends and family inside were having such a great time. She was in no rush to close that down, but right now what she really needed was some fresh air and a break from hosting… and a break from arguing.

"Room for another?" a familiar voice said from around the corner.

Heather scooched over a little, making room for Dale to join her. As he sat down, he felt just how freezing the night had become, but he didn't mind. He was willing to brace it for a few moments alone with her.

"How did you know I was out here?"

2.4: The Porch

Dale took a seat next to her, his ears ringing from the music.

"You always do this at parties. For as long as I can remember, you'd sit on the pavement outside, or in the garden, anywhere that was out of view."

"You knew?" she said. In all their years together, he'd never let on.

"Why do you think nobody ever came to bother you? Whenever we had people over, I could always tell when your battery started running low. I'd see you excuse yourself and disappear outside for half an hour or so. I'd watch the door, and if anyone started heading that way, I'd intercept them with small talk. You *know* how much I suck at small talk! But I knew all you needed was to sit and watch the stars for a while, then you'd come back fully recharged and be the life of the party again."

Her mind was flooded with fond memories as she thought back to all the times he must've known, all the times he'd helped her relax without her even knowing it. She smiled, a genuine one that she hadn't been sure she was capable of anymore.

"Then why are you bothering me now?" she joked.

"Well... I wanted to make sure you were okay. And also to give you your present."

"Another one? But you already gave me a banana!" She began laughing again, thinking back to her half-told story. "Oh hun, that day was so funny. THE YELLOW CAR, we kept saying, YELLOW LIKE A BANANA."

2.4: The Porch

"Then he came bounding back with a banana and a toy car, looking as confused as we did!"

The two laughed together again, the sort of quiet laugh you only get from a couple who are as connected as two people can be. Dale passed her another gift, wrapped in the same messy blue paper as the others.

"Oh my goodness," Heather said with genuine surprise as she ripped open the paper. It was a first edition print of *A Diary of Him, Her & Coffee*, her favourite book. "Dale, this is… I mean this…" She struggled to find the words. Instead, she leant in for a hug. "Thank you so much. So, *so* much!"

"Do you know how many years I've wanted to get this for you? Every birthday, anniversary, Christmas… I couldn't find it for love nor money. Luckily, nowadays it's not that rare… yet! You better hang onto that."

"I love it, Dale. Thank you." She clutched the book close to her chest, close to her heart. It really meant a lot to her.

"Heather, I'm…" For the second time that night, Dale said words that rarely left his mouth. "I'm really sorry."

"Whatever for?"

"For bailing on you at, you know…" He took a deep breath before he could say it. "Aiden's birthday. I feel so bad about that. We had all these nice plans, to go to that park he loved, go for pizza, celebrate *him*. But it was just too hard. The more I thought about it, the more it felt morbid. I'm sorry."

Heather held back a tear. "Dale, if you hadn't cancelled, I think I would have. All day I just wanted to call you."

2.4: The Porch

"Me too. Nobody else understood what it was like. How do you explain to somebody that it's the birthday of a child that doesn't exist here?"

Heather leant into Dale's shoulder. "I used to tell people about it all... But after a while, I got fed up with them looking at me like I was crazy."

"I know what you mean," Dale said. "I got fed up with the same attempts at trying to explain what it was. What was it that quack called it? 'A shared hallucinogenic event caused by a chemical concoction of heat, food, alcohol, and sunscreen.' A shared déjà vu, where one of us spoke of an event and the other felt it as if it were real."

"It wasn't that though, was it, Dale?"

"No, it wasn't that." Dale wrapped his arm around her, as she leant her head against his.

They shared a moment of silence as they looked up at the stars. Heather loved the stars. Whenever she felt overwhelmed by life, she would stare at the sky and imagine the scale of the universe. She'd imagine all the people in the houses around the world, living their lives just like she was. She'd imagine how small Earth was compared to the sun, the galaxy, the universe. She'd imagine her life, and how short it was compared to the length of all existence. All of it made her feel so tiny, so cosmically insignificant... there was no greater comfort to her. As she reflected on her small place within the vast universe, she sipped her tea, its warmth was as comforting as the stars.

2.4: The Porch

"Hey," Dale said, noticing she was using a drink for heat. He released her, then looked her up and down. "You're not smoking?"

"I've given up... properly this time."

"Good on you."

"You know how much I battled to give up before, in our other life, I mean. I kept trying and failing and being disappointed in myself. I couldn't face that constant battle again. I decided to make a choice – either smoke forever and stop being so hard on myself, or give up while I'm still young enough to be able to easily. Well, relatively easily. So that's what I'm doing. It's been four months now."

"Lynn would be so proud," Dale said, without thinking. He choked on the words as they left his throat.

"Hey, where's Anna?" Heather asked abruptly, not wanting to dwell on the thought of her daughter. "I keep wanting to talk to her tonight, but I get the feeling she doesn't like me very much."

"She just doesn't know you here. You know it takes her a while to warm to people. She's in there." Dale gestured towards the noise inside. "Last time I saw her, she was chatting to your sister. She's gonna be pissed that I've come out here and left her."

"Well, good luck with that." Heather raised her eyebrows.

"Oh, guess what?" Dale beamed. "So I took Anna to see *Apocalypse Cancelled* last week. She was so excited; I didn't have the heart to tell her I'd already seen it a million times."

2.4: The Porch

"I don't think I could watch it again," she joked.

"So we're getting to the end, right, with the big prime minister's speech. And I'm watching Anna's face to see how she reacts to the twist—"

"Was she shocked? I bet she screamed."

"It didn't happen!" Dale said, still as surprised now as he was in the cinema.

"What?"

"The big shootout outside Number Ten, it didn't happen. It just ends with the speech, then the credits roll. It's the weirdest thing."

Heather put her mug down on the porch, then looked at Dale, as equally confused as he was. "What? Why is it different? *How* is it different?"

"I've been racking my brain to work that out. How did my brother surviving that accident change the mind of some writer or director or editor thousands of miles away? I know someone he went to school with went on to film college, and I think they ended up moving to the states. Maybe Jak had some conversation with her that changed something? I don't know."

"Did you ask Jak about it?"

"Nah. We don't talk much these days. Things between us are… different."

"Oh, that's a shame," Heather said. It hadn't occurred to her before how their vision might've impacted his relationship with Jak. She decided not to press it.

2.4: The Porch

"You know what I wish?" she said. "I wish we'd played the lottery more. Not even for the money, more just to shut people up."

"Right? Whenever I've told people about the vision, that's the first thing they ask about!"

The two gently laughed together before slipping back into a comfortable silence.

"It's all so weird, isn't it?" Heather muttered. Suddenly, her voice picked up. "Oh, this'll make you laugh! I've been offered a temp job over at Grovers, covering a three-month project. If only they knew—"

"Don't take it," he said, abruptly interrupting her. "You did, what, twenty-eight years with Grovers? Do you really want to go back to that?"

"I wasn't going to, I just thought it was funny. I forgot all about it only being a three-month initial contract. The problem is, being a business analyst is the only thing I know how to do. I feel like we've got this opportunity to do things again, but I don't know where to start."

Dale took her hand. "You should write."

She rolled her eyes. "You know I would if I could."

He started rubbing her hand with his fingers, the same way she always used to do for him. "You can. Think of it like your smoking. How many times did you start something and not finish it? Hundreds? Just take some time out and write. You always said you had problems seeing it through, but I think it was fear of putting yourself out there. But now we know how fragile life is. Promise me you'll try, Heather. What have you got to lose that we haven't already lost?"

2.4: The Porch

She turned and looked him in the eye. "I promise."

Their eyes stayed locked for a little longer than either intended. Both contemplated leaning in for a kiss, but just as Dale was about to, Heather pulled back and quickly continued the conversation.

"What about you, Dale? Are you working for your mum yet?"

"Nah... I did that long enough. Jak can take over the business this time."

"Then what will you do?"

Dale smiled towards the stars. "I have absolutely no idea."

There was a collective joyful scream from inside the house, and then the music got *even* louder. For a moment, they had both forgotten the party was even happening.

"I should head back in soon." Heather feigned preparing to get up and go, but they both knew she wasn't ready yet. "I need to check on Lyndon."

"How's he doing?"

"It's been... tough. Me and you, Dale, we had a rhythm to everything. To life. And now I'm getting frustrated at Lyndon all the time as he isn't in that same rhythm. But that's on me, I've changed it, so I know it's not fair. Before that holiday we had our own thing going. But now it feels broken. He feels the frustration too, but he's patient. I wouldn't say understanding. How can anyone understand this thing? But patient, at least."

"That's something, I guess."

2.4: The Porch

Heather accepted that she wasn't going anywhere yet and relaxed onto the porch, lying on her back so she could look up at the stars better. Dale did the same, taking his place next to her, his hands behind his head to stop it resting on the cold concrete.

"How are you, Dale? Honestly?"

"I'm trying to take it one day at a time. But honestly... I'm not good. I miss *them* so much."

Dale remained dry eyed, as he always did, but his words had an impact on Heather. She tried to hide it, but the tears rolled down her face and into her hair beneath.

Dale continued, "I feel like they're here, with me, all the time. Every day I wake up and I have this split second of... not forgetting things, that's not right, I haven't forgotten... but I have this flicker, like my mind thinks they're still here and I can go see them. Sometimes I'll even reach for my phone to call them. But then the moment goes, and reality hits again. And I can't talk about it because nobody understands. I know it sounds horrible, but sometimes I think at least..." He paused, losing his nerve.

Heather wiped her eyes with her sleeve. "Say it."

"At least if they'd been here, in this life, and they'd died, people would understand our grief, you know?"

"I know," she said through the sobbing. "My heart is broken. It's never going to be fixed. Every time I close my eyes I see Lynn's face, smiling at some crass joke she made and watching us all squirm. Or Aiden when he got excited about some dumb movie. Even though he knew we didn't care, he was excited to share it with us all the same. But when I talk to people about it, I feel like I have to constantly justify my pain."

Dale rested his head on the floor and reached his arm under Heather. She rolled into him and wrapped her arms around him, closing her eyes as she rested her head on his shoulder. She could feel his heart pounding so hard that it seemed as if it could burst right through his rib cage at any moment. They both knew that feeling well; they'd gotten used to it over the last year.

"It's all just so hard," Heather said, stroking his chest.

"It's not just them… I miss you too, Heather. I know you said you needed time, and I'm trying so hard not to push that, I really am. But I can't take only seeing you every few weeks, having to hold back what I really want to say."

Heather wiped her tears again, then tilted her head to look him in the eye. "Dale, please…"

"I know, I know. But it's been months, and every time I see you it gets harder. I miss you so fucking much."

"I miss you too," she sighed, all the tension leaving her muscles. "I feel like we've been given this second life, a chance to do it all over again. I'm trying to understand what that means, and not jump into anything without thinking it through. I'm trying to do what's right, for me, for you, for Lyndon. It's all so confusing, isn't it?"

"Not for me. I know how I feel when I'm with you, and I know how I feel when I'm not. Everything else around that is just noise. For me, it's very simple. This, right now, being with you… It's the best I've felt in ages. And I feel this way *every* time we're together. And I think, I *hope*, it's the same

2.4: The Porch

for you. There is nothing complicated about that. Doesn't it feel like we're meant to be together?"

Heather rested her hand on his face, stroking it gently with her thumb. The warmth of his body next to hers was all consuming, even through the freezing air. She looked into his eyes, really looked this time. Those eyes carried so much history, so much pain, so much love. It was just the two of them and the stars, in the first moment of true peace either had felt in such a long time.

"I think you might be right, Dale."

Part 3
The Wedding
5 years after the vision

3.1: The Drive

The car sputtered at every roundabout, every stop sign, every traffic light, but the old banger was still functioning, and that was all that mattered. Dale knew he was on borrowed time. He'd botched it where he could, managed to keep it running, but soon he'd have no choice but to do something about it. He couldn't afford to get it fixed but he couldn't afford *not* to have a car, either. At some point, something was going to have to give.

Dale had vowed he'd never drive after Jak's accident, but events over the past few years had made it essential. The car was probably well overdue for retirement even when Dale bought it. He was praying it would survive this journey. He made himself a promise – if it made it there and back again without completely blowing up, he'd find some way to get it sorted properly. He cursed himself every time the engine popped, or the exhaust rattled, knowing he really should have looked it over more carefully before setting off. But it was too late for that now; the wedding was tomorrow, and he had a long way to go. One hundred and sixty miles, to be exact, back to the place he once called home. Back to New Oxford.

How long had it been since he was last back there? Five months? Maybe six? He wasn't sure. He'd originally planned to be there a week before the wedding, then a few days, at least a couple of days… but he'd left it to the last minute, as

3.1: The Drive

he always did. Luckily the motorway was quiet the whole way; the last thing he needed was to keep stop-starting in that heap. The drive seemed to disappear a lot quicker than he'd expected – there had been times before when it would just drag on and on, the inescapable tedium of being alone in his car with nothing but miles of dull road ahead. Thankfully, this wasn't one of them.

He took the slip road as he spotted the sign for New Oxford. He wasn't sure how he'd feel going back. He'd run the scenario several times through his mind along the way – would he be excited, nervous, angry? The answer was one thing he hadn't predicted. He felt nothing. Numb.

It was a feeling he knew only too well – a feeling he'd become familiar with over recent years. It was as if he'd blown an emotional fuse, and having had to decide between feeling everything or feeling nothing, he'd opted for the latter.

The traffic lights in the city turned red as he approached and Dale was reminded of how they always used to catch him out. He swore they could sense him coming and would deliberately change, the city's way of inconveniencing him.

As he pulled up to the third set, deep in the city centre, he spotted something out of the corner of his eye. Just outside his passenger door was a small independent bookshop. The window was plastered with a bright sign shouting about a new book launch from a local author. Dale didn't look any closer – he didn't need to; he knew what it said. That didn't stop the temptation. It took all his strength

3.1: The Drive

not to glance over, even though he knew it wouldn't do him any good to see it. He was there for the wedding, that was his focus, nothing else mattered. He told himself that over and over, but he still wasn't sure he believed it. *Come on, lights*. The temptation to look grew. The sign in the bookshop seemed to get brighter, gnawing at his brain, screaming for him to acknowledge it. *Come on, lights!!*

He needed a distraction. He pulled down the rear-view mirror and stared at himself. How long had it been since he'd shaved? A month? Maybe more? He told himself he had to do it before the big event. The sign clawed intensely at his skin. The distraction wasn't working – he could still feel it tugging on his ear, trying to forcibly turn his head. He held strong until, finally, he was set free. The lights turned green and he continued on, deep into a city that held two lifetimes of memories.

3.2: The Day Before

Dale let out all the air in his lungs before knocking on the door. It was a door he hadn't knocked on in a while, much longer than it should've been. He caught himself in the reflection of the glass panel and realised just how scruffy he looked. The knees on his jeans were faded, a day or two at most from splitting completely. The arms on his hoodie were frayed, his trainers grubby, and his T-shirt had gained sweat patches during the drive. In his defence, he'd been on the road since 5am – still, he knew he should've made more of an effort. At least the sun was shining; if it was like this tomorrow, the wedding would be glorious. He could hear voices inside. They were talking so loudly he doubted they heard him at the door. Dale knocked again, harder this time.

"Door's open!" a female voice shouted, not the one he was expecting.

Dale let himself in and went straight for the lounge.

"Wow," he said as soon as he entered the room. She stood there, in an elegant, flowing white dress, a true vision of beauty. "You scrub up alright, Anna."

"Dale!" she shrieked. She waddled over to him, the best she could in the constricting dress, and wrapped her arms around him.

"Hey! Don't wrinkle the dress!" Jess shouted from the sofa across the other side of the room. Dale hadn't even noticed her there. Jess was an old friend of theirs from school, though Dale had no idea when he last saw her. She

3.2: The Day Before

wasn't someone he kept in contact with. Actually, other than Anna, he didn't keep in contact with any of their old group.

"Let me go change, then we'll head out," Anna said, letting go of her friend. She lifted the train, then shuffled out of the room and proceeded carefully, *very carefully*, up the staircase.

Jess pushed aside the stack of papers she had on her lap. From what Dale could tell, they were a bunch of handwritten notes to do with the wedding. She got up from the sofa, and the two exchanged a polite cheek-kiss.

"Alright Dale, how's things? Happy to be back home again?"

He wasn't home. Not anymore.

"I'm fine, you know. Are you coming to this dinner thing tonight?"

"Of course. Make sure you get her there by seven, okay?" Jess paused and looked Dale up and down. "Actually, I know what you're like. Maybe you should aim for half six."

"Don't worry, we'll be there."

There were a series of thumps as Anna came bounding back down the stairs, this time in her jeans and hoodie too, though hers were showing much less wear and tear.

"Are you sure you're okay to set up the chair covers?" Anna asked Jess.

"Yes, don't worry, I'll head over to the church now."

Church? Dale knew Anna wasn't religious; he'd assumed it would be in a registry office.

3.2: The Day Before

"And the caterers," Anna continued, "they want to move…"

"They want to move the meat in today," Jess pre-empted her. "Don't worry, Anna, I've got it. Everything is going to go smoothly."

"Thanks, Jess. You're the best."

The two hugged. When had Anna become such a hugger? And when had she and Jess become so close? They were friends, sure, but Dale couldn't remember Anna getting on any more with Jess than she did the rest of their old group. And yet, there she was helping with the wedding preparations.

Had he really been gone that long?

The duo walked together into the city's shopping centre, something they hadn't done in far too long. They both missed it, though Dale hadn't realised just how much until he was actually there. Anna was a little disappointed that her best friend had left it so close before coming down for her wedding, but she had consciously decided not to dwell on that. He was there now, and that was all that mattered. All she wanted to do in that moment was drag Dale to Waffle On and have a proper catch-up, but there was no time for that. There was still much to do for the big day. At least they could chat on the walk.

"So come on, Dale. How's life up north? Tell me everything!"

"There's not much to tell," Dale replied, not untruthfully, "I'm still working on the same building site. They've got more

3.2: The Day Before

work than people so everyone is rushing things more than they should be, which makes my job of keeping on top of the health and safety a nightmare. But at least I know the work won't dry up anytime soon. The actual town is... fine, I guess. No complaints. It's quieter than here."

"Wow, Dale," she said sarcastically. "Calm down, it sounds so exciting."

Dale struggled to talk about his life at the best of times, but he really didn't have much to say. He lived alone, he worked alone, he had a routine. It wasn't good or bad, it just *was*.

"Anyway," he said, "today is about you. You're getting married tomorrow! Has it sunk in yet? Are you ready?"

Anna stared at the pavement in a moment of contemplation. She hadn't stopped smiling since Dale had arrived. "I've been ready to marry Bob since about a month after we met."

"Where is the future Mr Anna today?"

"He's super traditional – hence the church and the whole 'can't see the bride before the wedding day' thing – so he's staying with a friend. They're having a wild night of their own; an evening of filing tax returns."

Dale grinned in a way that he hadn't done since he left New Oxford. "My guess is they'll be in bed with a cup of hot cocoa by seven, lights off by half past."

The two laughed together, sharing a moment of rekindled connection.

3.2: The Day Before

They reached the first destination on their list – Halbjorns, a tiny upmarket clothing store specialising in suit hire for men. Dale was trying on a suit that Anna had picked for him: a navy blue three-button jacket with matching trousers, salmon waistcoat, golden pocket square, and a tie-thing that he had no idea how to wear. Anna and the store owner had taken a step back to get a full view of Dale in the suit and were busy discussing the fit. The size wasn't perfect, but it was as close as they were going to get; it was too late now to get one properly tailored.

"That'll do fine. Thanks, Halbjorn," Anna said.

"Do you want to take it now?"

"We'll come and grab it in a couple of hours if that's okay? We've got a few other bits to do before then. Dale, I assume you're getting changed at your mum's tomorrow?"

Dale pulled at the cuffs of the jacket. They weren't too short, but he wasn't used to wearing something that wasn't baggy. "Oh, I'm not staying at Mum's."

"What? Where are you staying then?"

"At the Sleep'n'save."

Anna scrunched up her face. "At that grotty shithole? Why?" The answer became clear in his face. "Dale... your mum and Jak know you're back, right?"

"I'm not staying long."

What he meant was he wasn't staying long enough to see them. Anna didn't push it; she had too much to sort and she didn't want to upset her friend. The shopkeeper

3.2: The Day Before

signalled to Dale that he was done and needed the suit back. Dale disappeared into the changing room.

"Do you like the suit?" Anna asked, talking through the curtain.

"I think so… I'm not used to wearing one. You sure I don't look a bit of a twat?"

"Course you do," she said, "but it's a wedding. We'll all look a bit of a twat. Seriously though, it's alright, yeah? The suit?"

Dale could tell that it was important to her that he liked it. "Yeah, it's nice." *Nice. That wasn't going to cover it.* "It's *really* nice… it's got more colour than I expected. I'd have thought Bob would've picked something grey… with a grey tie and grey shoes."

Anna snorted a little, caught off guard.

"I told Bob I wanted at least three colours in there, that was his challenge."

Anna heard shuffling inside the curtain, slow shuffling, like he was being careful not to damage the suit.

"Don't go wasting money on me though, Anna. I told you I've already got a suit I can wear."

"Not that pinstripe one Margaret bought you when we were like, nineteen?"

"Yeah…"

"Dale!" Anna exclaimed. "That was too small for you even back then. Anyway, I want you to match the wedding party tomorrow."

"Why?"

3.2: The Day Before

"Well…" – Anna moved a little closer to the changing room – "Look, you know my father has long gone. And most… well, *all* my family are a sack of shit."

"That's putting it nicely," Dale said, knowing she'd take it well.

"So I was thinking… I was hoping… that you'd give me away tomorrow."

The curtain swung open to reveal Dale wearing nothing but a pair of bright-white boxer shorts, the suit trousers still attached to one leg.

"Are you serious?"

"You don't have to do anything. Just walk down the aisle with me and stand at the front looking like a twat while we do our vows."

Dale leant forward and wrapped his arms around his friend. "I'd be honoured, Anna."

"Okay, great, but maybe put some clothes on first…" she said, ushering him back into the changing room and yanking the curtain closed.

Once the suit was done, the duo moved onto Gallodays to check the centre pieces had been delivered to the hotel, Matridance to confirm the music selection, then they took a much-needed break at Starbucks to grab a coffee. It had only recently opened, which was obvious given how modern it looked compared with the rest of the stores on the street.

"It's no Waffle On," Dale joked, looking around at the sterile floors and clean tables.

3.2: The Day Before

"Trust me, if it wasn't all the way across town, that's where I'd have taken you."

Dale took a sip of his coffee. "Yuk," he said sarcastically. "It feels weird being able to actually taste it."

"Right," Anna was keen to get right back to business, "Next up, I want to check the cake is on track for tomorrow."

"Oh, what sort of cake is it?"

"Bob picked it, so it's a vanilla sponge with 'It is a wedding' written on top."

Dale's shoulders bounced in a way they only did with his friend. The feeling took him right back to being a teenager again.

"I've missed this, Anna."

"Taking the piss out of Bob?"

"No, I mean just you and me hanging out."

"Me too. How are you, really, Dale? You seem… I don't know. Distant? I mean, you were always sort of distant. But this time it feels different. Before you were a bit lost, now it's like you're gone completely."

"I'm fine. I'm going from one day to the next." He took a deep breath. "Have you read it?" he asked quietly.

"Read what?"

"The book. *The* book."

"Ah…" Anna's face dropped as she realised what he meant. "No, I haven't. I don't want to. No good can come of it."

Dale nodded, then quickly changed the subject.

3.2: The Day Before

"What about you, Anna? How are you? You seem excited about tomorrow."

"I am... I think. I know all this stuff we're doing today has already been checked a hundred times, I know it'll all be fine, but I just want to check it again. I'm anxious."

"About what?"

"I want it to be perfect for Bob. He's put so much time and money into this. He did most of the organising, too. Almost *all* of it, actually. I was happy to go down to the town hall or something, just the two of us. But he asked for this, a bigger, more traditional wedding. And Bob rarely asks me for anything. I just... I don't want to disappoint him."

"You could never do that," Dale reassured her, placing his hand on hers.

"Most of the guests going are his. I didn't realise how many people he was friends with until we did the guest list. All I have is a handful of people from work and some of the old gang."

"Is..." Dale wasn't sure if he should ask, but he had to know. "Will Heather be going?"

"What?" Anna pulled her hand away. "No, of course not. Why would she be?"

"I don't know, I just wanted to check."

Anna rolled her eyes. "Dale, I don't know her. And even if I did, do you think I'd want her there now? After all she's done?"

"I guess not."

3.2: The Day Before

Dale stared out the window at nothing in particular. He just stared, fumbling his coffee cup with his thumbs as he lost himself in thought.

Anna knew the look well.

"You haven't contacted her, have you?"

"No… but…"

"No *buts* Dale. You can't. It won't bring you anything but pain, you know that."

"I know…" He shook himself out of his trance. "But we're family, you know? We should be married by now, we should have our children…"

"Don't do this, Dale," Anna said firmly. "Not again."

3.3: The Night Before

"It's not a hen party," Anna insisted.

The duo arrived at Carlucios, the best Italian restaurant in the city, half an hour early to get the table ready. They'd been given a private room away from the main restaurant, much to Anna's surprise. The room was well lit with scatterings of LED candles. The stone walls were decorated with hanging pots and pans, rows of authentic olive oil bottles sat atop wooden shelves, and the table was decorated with a red-and-white chequered cloth.

"Of course it isn't a hen party," Dale said, scattering some sparkly wedding confetti over the table. "It's just a gathering of close friends the night before the wedding, and Bob isn't allowed to come."

"It's just a…" Anna paused to think of the words. "A pre-wedding friendly dinner."

"Oh, okay." Dale winked. "Who else is coming?"

Anna put down the banner she was holding and began counting on her fingers as she recalled the names, being careful not to miss anybody.

"There's me, you, Jess, and Rob."

Both were friends of theirs from school.

"Terri, who I work with, and her husband, Ian. Umm…" Anna stared at her fingers, knowing there were more. "Oh, Zoe's coming."

3.3: The Night Before

"Oh cool," Dale said. Zoe was Bob's sister. Even though she was older than him, she always seemed much more youthful. She was a bit of a punk, in every positive sense of the word. She was covered head to toe in tattoos, her hair a different colour and style every time they saw her. Anna often joked about how Zoe took all the personality when she was born, leaving none for Bob.

Anna twisted her nose as she got to the final name.

"And this Shyla woman."

"Who?"

"She works with Bob." Now that she was done counting, she picked up the *Getting Married* banner and returned to blue-tacking it to the wall. "It's weird, I don't really know her at all, I've only met her a couple of times. But she got married a few months ago and she invited me to her, ummm…"

"Pre-wedding friendly dinner?" Dale joked.

"Yeah. So I kinda felt like I had to."

"Fair enough."

Dale had finished sprinkling the confetti, the banners were up, and Anna had opened a couple of bottles of house wine in preparation for guests arriving.

"What next?" Dale asked enthusiastically. She hadn't said it, but Dale got the feeling that this task, preparing the room, was something she would have asked him to do if he'd come back to New Oxford sooner. He kept putting it off, until she had no choice but to handle it all herself.

3.3: The Night Before

"Just sit there," she said, signalling to one of the chairs. "I want to visualise it."

She reached into her bag and pulled out a stack of folded white cards, each bearing a handwritten name. She began to place them around the table.

"Do you want to sit next to Jess or Rob?"

"God, not Rob," Dale blurted without thinking. "Can't I sit next to you?"

"Yeah, you are, but on the other side of you?" Anna was confused by his reaction to Rob. As far as she knew, the two had always got on well, but she decided to ignore it. Instead, she sat Jess on the other side of him.

She placed the last card down, then took a seat at the head of the table.

"Shall we just sack this off and go get waffles?" she said, the anxiety of the impending evening creeping in.

"I don't think Waffle On has ever had eight customers at once."

"We can sack them all off too."

Dale smiled – thinking about that dingy cafe brought back so many memories.

"I tell you what," he said, "as soon as you're back from your honeymoon, we'll grab waffles. It's been too long. You can even invite Bob."

"I don't think he's ever even seen a waffle," Anna joked.

She began twisting her hair with a finger, as if building up to say something. "Anyway, when I'm back from my honeymoon, I'm gonna be pretty busy."

3.3: The Night Before

"Oh?" Dale tried to read her face but came up blank.

"I, uh... I start my training next month."

"No way! As an officer? Really?"

She smiled and nodded, deservedly proud of herself.

"Well why the hell didn't you tell me before?" He leant forward and wrapped his arms around her. They'd hugged more that day than they had in years.

"I wanted to tell you in person."

"That's fantastic, Anna."

Dale leant across the table and grabbed a bottle of wine. Neither of them genuinely liked wine, but it felt like the right time for it. He poured them both a glass – a *small* glass – then lifted his up. "To the police finally seeing sense and giving you a shot."

Anna raised her glass and knocked his. "To no more shitty jobs," she said.

The two took a sip of their wine, then simultaneously winced and placed the glasses back on the table, never to be touched again.

The other guests arrived in dribs and drabs over the next hour. They drank, they ate, they laughed. Anna, in particular, hadn't stopped laughing the whole evening. Dale had expected that she'd find the whole thing overwhelming, much in the way he did. Neither of them could be in a large group for long before needing to take some time alone. Well, alone together. The duo would normally find some excuse to leave, then go and hang out together to recharge. At least,

3.3: The Night Before

that's how Dale remembered it from when they were younger, but this night was different. Anna seemed so at ease with everyone, and she fully engaged with every topic being bounced around the table.

Much of the conversation was being led by Ian, the husband of Anna's work friend, Terri. He didn't really know anyone else there and was one of the most removed from the group. At first glance, with his thick glasses, skinny cheeks, and general nerdish appearance, you'd think he was the quiet type. And yet, he had been so quick to work out who everyone was and find what made them laugh. Dale was in awe of Ian's confidence. Envious, even.

"My name isn't actually Ian," he said, laughing in preparation for yet another story.

Terri rolled her eyes, as if she knew what was coming.

"This is genuinely true." He shuffled onto his elbows, excited to get into the details. "My name is actually Terry."

"Wait, what?" Anna said abruptly, laughing across the table. "You're Terry and Terri?"

"When I was younger, I used to work in a cafe," Ian started, "and this beautiful woman used to come in every day and order the same thing: a cappuccino and a bagel. Every single day, without fail. And she was, you know, truly stunning."

His wife smiled sweetly.

"And one day, I finally plucked up the courage to ask her to move out the way so that I could serve Terri." He winked at his wife as she scoffed. "But seriously, one day I asked her what her name was, and she said 'Terri'. I was so nervous that I panicked. I thought if I told her my name was Terry, too, she'd think I was winding her up and I'd ruin it. So I told her my name was Ian, which is my middle name."

"No way," Zoe shouted, the alcohol adding extra *oomph* to her voice.

"How long was it until he told you the truth?" Anna asked Terri.

"Six months," Terri said.

A simultaneous chorus of "*Six months*?!" was heard around the table.

"Jesus, Ian!" Anna exclaimed.

"Even then," Terri continued, "it was only because I saw it on his bank card! But I thought it was kinda cute. Well, not at first... but after he explained it all."

"So what do you call him?" Anna asked.

"That idiot, usually," Ian replied.

The whole table laughed. Even Dale, uncomfortable as he was to have been with so many people for so long, quietly joined in with the rest.

"When I met my partner," Rob said, "I told them my name was Robert De Niro, as a joke."

"Of course you did," Dale snapped from across the table. It was just like Rob to try and one-up someone else's story. Dale had hardly said a word all night. He'd answered any questions that were directed his way, but otherwise he kept much to himself and just observed. Now though, his snide remark had brought with it an uncomfortable silence that lay thick across the table.

3.3: The Night Before

"Now that I think about it, I'm pretty sure Terri was only coming into the cafe every day to try and get my number anyway," Ian (or Terry) joked, once again lifting the atmosphere.

"That is not true!" Terri shouted. "The coffee there was amazing."

The two continued. The rest of the table watched, anticipating the next punch line. But not Dale. His attention was pulled in another direction as Anna subtly, then again *not* so subtly, kicked him under the table. He looked over and gestured, as if to say *What?*

"What's going on with you and Rob?" she whispered. "You've been weird with him all night."

"It's nothing... I didn't even know you two were still friends."

"We hang out sometimes."

"The three of you?" he asked, signalling to Jess. "I thought the old group had pretty much gone."

"It had, but these last couple of years we've started seeing each other a bit more."

Dale felt something come over him, something it took a few moments to identify. Jealousy. But although he knew *what* it was, he wasn't sure he knew *why*. Was it because the old group had half reformed without him? He quickly dismissed that; outside of Anna, he'd never been particularly close to any of them. He hadn't thought she was either. Maybe that was where the jealousy stemmed from?

3.3: The Night Before

"Anyway, it's irrelevant. Tell me what's going on with Rob," she insisted.

"You won't get it." He could tell from her stare that she wasn't going to let it go. "He screwed me over…" Dale scanned the rest of the table to make sure nobody else was in earshot. They were all too engrossed in the tales from the two Terries to care about the whispering. "We talked about this idea of buying stock art, printing it on shirts, then selling them. Then a couple of years later, he went and did it with some guy he worked with. They completely cut me out."

"What are you talking about? When was this?" Her whisper was heavier than before, sharper.

"In about five or six years' time… in, you know, the other life."

"For fuck's sake, Dale," she said. "You can't be pissy at him for something he hasn't actually done."

"I knew you wouldn't understand."

Anna shook her head in disapproval, then turned her attention back to the group. Her smile snapped on instantly, as if it had never left.

Dale downed the remainder of his beer, then signalled the waiter to bring another.

"I said I wouldn't drink too much. Big day tomorrow," Anna addressed the group. Everyone had just finished desserts, and Shyla, the woman Bob worked with, had insisted that Anna do a speech. She was reluctant at first, but soon the peer pressure came at her from all angles. "But I just want to

3.3: The Night Before

thank you all for coming tonight. It really means the world to me. I can't believe I'm getting married tomorrow. I've known Bob for many years now, and no matter how messy life gets, how unstable, he's always there by my side. I feel so lucky to have met such a wonderful man." Anna choked a little as she spoke, the alcohol and the events of the evening bringing her emotions to the surface.

"He's the lucky one!" Zoe shouted across the table.

"Thanks, Zoe." Anna's already stretched smile somehow grew even wider. "This will be my last drink, I need to make sure I can actually get up in the morning, but I'd like to raise a toast" – she raised her glass high into the air – "to all of you for sharing this with me, and to Bob, even though he's not here tonight."

"And to you, sis!" Zoe added. "One of the best and… umm… loveliest people in the world! To Anna and Bob!"

"To Anna and Bob!" the group shouted as they knocked glasses.

All, except Dale.

He had remained still, flat, emotionless throughout the speech. It wasn't from a lack of caring, he'd just had a little too much, and now his mind was descending too fast for him to grab hold. He knew he should stop, but the more the night had gone on, the lonelier he felt. The more it felt like something, or *someone*, was missing. It wasn't Anna's fault, it wasn't any of their faults, but knowing that wasn't helping the fact. After all, Anna had been a big part of *their* wedding, even if she didn't know it.

3.3: The Night Before

As soon as the speech was over, he finished his drink, then proceeded towards the bar for a refill.

"Hey, Dale," Jess said from behind him. He hadn't even noticed her follow him to the bar. "What's going on with you?"

"What do you mean?" Dale's head was fuzzier than he realised – standing up had been a mistake.

"You're, I dunno, quiet and snappy. You don't seem yourself. Is it…" She paused for a moment, as if unsure if she should continue. Suddenly, she found the courage to go for it. "Is it because of that book?"

"You read it?" Dale whipped around to face her.

She nodded, doing the best impression of a sympathetic look that the alcohol would allow.

"Fuck," Dale said.

The look grew deeper, more tragic, more genuine. "If it's true, all that, then it's fucked up, and I'm sorry you had to go through that. So… is it?"

"Is it what?"

"True? What she wrote?"

Dale stood silently for a second. He had both nothing and too much to say. He could hear the bartender behind him, fighting for his attention, but he couldn't move. He couldn't speak. He just stood.

"Dale?" Jess asked, moving up onto her toes to try to catch his eye.

"I've gotta go." Dale rushed towards the door. "Tell Anna I'll see her in the morning."

3.4: The Book

Dale stared at the flaking ceiling of his dingy hotel room. The morning light was just starting to break through the cheap floral curtains. He'd watched the whole night tick by, intending to sleep, *wanting* to sleep, but kept awake by swirling thoughts. At first it was the alcohol but as he sobered, he realised it was more than that. His mind was preoccupied, and the only way he was going to get any sort of release was to see *her*. He'd come all that way – how could he not see her?

He checked his watch: 8:04 a.m. She lived thirty minutes from the hotel. The wedding started at eleven – he had time.

He rolled out of bed and made the strongest coffee he could using every sachet the hotel had provided. After a quick rinse and a much-needed shave, he carefully put on the wedding suit, doing his best not to crease it.

9:27 a.m. Still plenty of time.

Dale drove across the city towards the other end of town. With each stop, his mind screamed at him to turn back. He knew it was a bad idea, he knew she wouldn't want to see him, but his thoughts were quashed by his determination. *Maybe it won't be too bad*, he thought. *Maybe this time it will be different, and we'll get our lives back on track, together.*

Deep down, he knew it was unlikely.

3.4: The Book

He parked opposite her townhouse and took a long, deep breath. He told himself this was a spur of the moment decision, that the discussions of the previous evening had pushed him into going to see her, but deep down he knew it was bullshit. As much as he denied it, to others, to himself, he knew he would end up going to see her. He'd obsessed over it for weeks leading up to the trip, barely thinking about anything else. The real reason he'd left it so late to come down for the wedding was because he knew the more time he had in New Oxford, the more likely he was to see her. If he was too busy, if he had no free time, then he wouldn't be able to. It was a sensible plan. A failed sensible plan.

His heart pounded heavier with each step towards the door. It'd been a while since he'd last seen her, too long. He knocked on the door, softer than he'd told his hand to do it, but it was still enough.

"Hang on!" a voice shouted from deep inside the house, a voice he knew well, a voice that reminded him of home.

The door swung open and there she stood. Curly brown hair, denim jacket, black leggings. He knew the look well. He knew the face well. He was wrong: she didn't remind him of home, she *was* home.

"Hey, Heather," he said sheepishly.

"No, no, Dale, no!" Her face became sharp when she saw him behind the door.

"Can we just talk?"

"No, we can't. I told you, no more phone calls, no more letters, and no more turning up at my house." The sharpness intensified with each word.

3.4: The Book

"I just want to talk. Five minutes, please, Heather," he begged.

"Goodbye, Dale."

She pulled the door, but it caught something before it could close. Dale had stuck his foot in the gap.

"Move your foot."

"I just want to talk."

"There's nothing else for us to say. Move your foot."

"No!" Dale shouted, a rare moment of actually demonstrating some emotion. "You need to talk to me, Heather. How could you do it? How could you write that book? How could you write about me, about our kids, about us?"

She sighed and closed her eyes, bracing herself for a conversation she'd hoped to avoid.

"I didn't use your name," she said through the gap in the door.

"That's hardly the point. You wrote our story. *Our* story. And you didn't even tell me. I know things aren't good between us, I know you want space, but you should have told me what you were doing. You owe me a conversation, Heather."

Dale removed his foot, giving her the chance to shut the door if she wanted. To his surprise, the door stayed static, the air silent. She slowly pulled it open just enough for Dale to walk in. They moved silently through the hallway and into the lounge. Heather signalled for Dale to sit on the sofa, then began moving some magazines off a wooden chair in the

3.4: The Book

corner of the room. Once clear, she pulled the chair adjacent to the sofa, then left the room. Still not a word was spoken, but Dale heard the clanking of cups and a kettle being boiled from the kitchen.

The lounge was smaller than he'd remembered; it must have been a year since he was last there. The glass-topped coffee table was littered with leaflets from estate agents – was she selling the place? It would make sense; she'd always wanted to get out of there and into somewhere bigger. Something else in the room caught his eye. Above the TV was a silver picture frame that hadn't been there before, containing a print of a book cover. The title, *What Could Have Been*, was written in big letters over a blue sea, accompanied by a boat that left a stream tearing apart the two realities. Just under the title was her name, Heather Wiley. Wiley, not Sawyer. That felt wrong. Dale got off the sofa, lifted the frame off its nail, and carefully placed it behind the TV out of sight.

Heather returned a few moments later, walking carefully so as not to spill the coffee.

"Thanks," Dale said, taking a mug from her. He pulled a coaster from under the leaflets and placed the mug down.

"What's with the suit?" Heather asked as she sat down in the wooden chair by the sofa. She wasn't used to seeing Dale dressed so smart. She hoped it wasn't for her sake.

"It's nothing. I've got a thing later."

"Oh…"

Heather leant forward and took a biro from under the table, then used the end of it to stir her coffee. She wasn't sure why. She'd never done that before, the coffee certainly didn't need stirring, but she felt like she had to do something with her hands, something to cut through the awkwardness. She knew what he had to say, but she didn't want to hear it.

"Heather, that book…"

"I'm sorry, Dale."

"For writing it? Or for not telling me?"

"For…" She paused as her eyes scanned the room, noticing something was missing and realising what Dale had done. She shook it off and moved her attention back to the man on her sofa. "I'm sorry for not telling you. And I'm sorry things between us have just been so… difficult, for these last couple of years. You're right, I should have told you what I was doing."

Dale scoffed. "But you're not sorry for writing it?"

"I *had* to write it. I had to do something with all that pain. I turned it into—"

"You turned it into a career," Dale said bitingly. "You monetised our grief."

"You're the one who told me I should write."

"Not about us! You put our kids on a page. Do you not feel any guilt for that? Do you not feel anything for them?"

"How dare you!" Heather screamed, enough to spill boiling coffee onto her lap. She didn't react to the pain. "Don't you *dare* suggest that I am hurting any less than you are. I don't believe for a second you actually think that of me. I think you're trying to hurt me, or get some sort of reaction. I'm trying to—"

3.4: The Book

Dale's frustration quickly matched hers. He cut her off, again. "You're trying to deny they exist."

"No, Dale, I'm trying to accept that they're gone! I'm trying to move on with my life. I'm trying to push for *something*."

"Push for what?"

"For anything," she said, calmer than before. She placed her coffee down on the table, then took a moment to recentre herself. "Everything we did, the life we had, it was wonderful, Dale. But we fell into a lot of it." She could see his face tighten in disagreement. "I don't mean *us*. I fell into my job. I accepted a temp position and I never left. You took over your mum's business, that was meant to be temporary, too, but it wasn't. We didn't plan to have kids, it just kinda happened and we rolled with it. So much of our lives were built around things we didn't push for. We just coasted into whatever came our way. I want to push this time."

"To be a writer?"

"To be something I've chosen. Writing that book was my choice. I was wrong not to tell you about it, I accept that, but I couldn't face the conversation. I was cowardly, and I'm sorry."

"Well, at least you finally got something finished. I hope it was worth it," Dale said bitterly, turning away from her to face the window.

"I get it. You have every right to be upset about the book. But I had to write it, Dale. I had to find a way to process what happened. It was too much to keep in my

3.4: The Book

head, I needed to work through it somehow, and writing it was the only way I knew."

"Did it work?" He looked back at her. She appeared as broken as he felt. "Did it make you feel better?"

Heather dipped her head, all the energy drained from her body. "No, not really. I'm in pain, Dale. I have been for a long time. I know you are too. But I'm trying." She choked a little as tears formed in the corners of her eyes.

Dale noticed and shuffled to the end of the sofa, gently taking hold of one of her hands.

"We had a good life, didn't we?"

"We really did."

"Then why aren't we together?"

Heather scoffed and rolled her eyes, taking her hand back. "We've been through this."

"It doesn't make sense. We could be so good together," he pleaded.

"We tried, Dale. For almost two years we tried. It didn't work. We were a mess. We argued more in those two years than we ever did in thirty-five."

"But it *can* work. We know it can, Heather. The universe showed us that it can. It showed us that we're *meant* to be together."

"Whatever happened, it showed us that it *could* have been possible. But we were never meant to see that, Dale. We, you and I, as a couple, as a family; it only worked in that specific scenario, it doesn't work here. Your brother being alive has shaped you differently. My experiences without you have shaped me differently. Us not being together has shaped us differently."

"We can be those people, Heather, I know we can."

"No, Dale, we can't. We tried. We pretended we were them again, and it didn't work. They're gone, Dale. We're gone. We can't get those versions of ourselves back."

He shook his head furiously, unable to process what he was hearing. "We can't just write off thirty-five years together."

Heather rubbed her hands over her face, as if she'd had this conversation a million times before. "I've not even been alive for that long."

"So now you're just the same as everyone else? Pretending we didn't have that time together?"

Heather sat tall in her chair, her voice becoming colder, more commanding as she spoke. "We had *one* day together, just one day. That day came loaded with thirty-five years of memories, but it was still just one day."

Dale clenched his arms in frustration. "Was it? What else are memories except a life?" He paused for a moment to think. "Tell me this, Heather, what did you have for breakfast? Can you remember? Does that memory feel any different to ours?" He wasn't giving her a second to answer. "How do you know that actually happened? How do you know it's not just a memory? All of time could have started this morning, or when I walked through that door, and everything else is just memories."

3.4: The Book

"That's not the same, Dale. I can go in the kitchen now and see the crumbs from my toast, I can see the plate. Those things exist."

"I exist!" he screamed. "I'm *here*. You can see me. I don't know why you're so determined to undermine what happened to us, what we had."

"I'm not, Dale. I'm trying to rationalise it. I need to get on with my life and you do too. We have to find a way to process it. We tried explaining it, that didn't work. We tried recreating it, that didn't work. So now we have to accept it for what it was and move on."

"You sound like Lynn." Dale forced a smile onto his face. He started to laugh as he thought back. "Remember how she used to talk about compartmentalising a problem? God, she used to get at you about it!"

"You *have* to stop doing that."

"What?" His smile dropped.

"Whenever we talk, whenever we're serious, you start reminiscing about *them* to try and get me to... I don't know, recapture old feelings. It's emotionally manipulative." Heather began tapping her pockets for her cigarettes, forgetting that she hadn't had them for years. The urge was creeping in, exacerbated by the stress.

"So I can't even talk about them now? Not even with you, the *only* person who understands what it was like? The only person who knows what we went through?"

"We can talk about them, Dale, of course we can. But you can't use them like that."

3.4: The Book

"Why not? You used their deaths to sell that fucking book."

Heather shot out of her seat, her face a shade he'd never seen before, anger seeping out of every pore.

"*This* is why we can't fucking talk! This is why I can't see you anymore, Dale! Please, just go." She pointed towards the door.

Dale knew he'd pushed it too far. She wouldn't even look at him as he walked towards the hallway, stopping just before he reached the front door.

"I'm sorry, Heather. I didn't want to argue today, I just wanted to see you. I know those couple of years we were together were rough, I know that. I'm not stupid. Things weren't good. But that doesn't mean they never will be. There's still something here, between us. After all we've been through together, I don't understand how you can just turn your feelings off like that."

Heather joined him in the hallway, tears rolling down her face quicker than she could dry them. She stood in front of him and took his hands, her fingers damp.

"I love you, Dale. Always in all ways. You are more important to me than anybody else in the world. I have never once turned my feelings off."

"Then what?"

"It's too hard. My heart breaks every time I look at you."

"What if..." Dale started. Heather turned to look away, knowing what was coming. He gripped her hands a little tighter. "Please, just listen for a second." She turned her attention back to him. "Heather, what if we are *meant* to be those people. If we can push through the difficult parts, maybe we can get back to who we are supposed to be. I believe we can."

"No, we can't, and I can't keep going around in circles about this. Things had to happen how they happened for that version of ourselves to exist. And now, we're not those people, and we're not really these ones either. We're a mix that shouldn't have happened. We saw things we shouldn't have seen. And now we're broken, and I'm doing what I can to keep going, to be *normal*. This *thing* that happened to us, I can't let it be all-consuming. I can't waste this life because we saw a glimpse of another one."

"This is where we've always seen things differently, Heather. What *could* have been. I didn't really understand what you meant when we were together, how you saw the vision between us, but there it is splashed across your book. What could have been. But you're wrong! What we saw, it was what *should* have been. We're in the wrong life."

"I'm exhausted, Dale. All the time, every day, I am just *done*. Maybe you're right," – her arms went limp, he was the only thing holding them up now – "maybe that's what we should have had. But we don't. All we have is where we are now, and I am trying to do what I can to live with that. The book was my way of saying what I needed to say so that I could close it and move on."

He let go of her arms. "That damn book," he scoffed, "the Heather I knew never would have written it."

3.4: The Book

She sat on the staircase opposite the door, her head dipped, barely enough energy to speak.

"Exactly. That's what I've been trying to tell you. I'm not *that* Heather. You have to mourn her, Dale. You have to let her go."

"I don't know if I can. I don't know if I can live without you." He knelt in front of her. "I don't want to."

"I think it's best you leave now. I wish we could be friends. But we tried, and all it did was bring us both pain. We have these scars, these *big* scars that we can't hide. I'm trying to learn to live with mine, but you keep picking at the scab, thinking it'll provide some sort of relief when all it really does is make it worse and stop it from healing."

"Can I ask you one thing?" Dale said.

Heather used all the energy she had to lift her head. There were no more tears, no emotion, she was just... lost. He took that as a *yes*.

"When we were together, this time, I mean, those couple of years, did you want it to work?" he asked.

"More than anything."

3.5: The Distance

Anna's house was a couple of miles from the hotel. A little too far for a casual walk, but Dale chose that option anyway. The crisp morning air helped clear his head, and the time gave him a chance to think. His hoodie and jeans were doing little to combat the cold, but he was grateful for that. He could always focus better when it was cold. What else could he do to get through to Heather? How could she not see that they were supposed to be together?

As he walked down the road Anna lived on, he saw her front door suddenly open. She walked out wearing a similar hoodie to his, though hers was drawn over her head. She shut the door, then sat on the porch, waiting for Dale to approach. *She must have noticed me out the window*, he thought. But she never once acknowledged he was there, she never once looked over to him. Her hood being up was a bad sign; that was something she only ever did when she was anxious. She'd once described it as closing off the edges of her vision, and making the world feel a little less big.

Dale's feet became heavier with each step, like he was moving through jelly. He knew he'd messed up. He approached the porch and attempted to join his friend.

"Don't sit down," she said without averting her eyes from her trainers, her voice the coldest he'd ever heard.

"Anna, I'm so sorry…" he said with practised sincerity.

"Where were you yesterday?"

3.5: The Distance

Dale closed his eyes and took the deepest breath his lungs would allow. "I went to see Heather, and things got intense…"

Anna jumped to her feet. Much of her face was hidden in the dark of her hood, but he could just about make out gritted teeth. "Is that what you're telling me, really?"

"Anna, I'm sorry, I really am. I know I screwed up. But, you know… it was Heather."

Without warning, Anna pushed Dale with both her hands. He stumbled backwards, only just able to catch his footing and stay on his feet.

"You fucking arsehole! I needed you, Dale. I needed you!"

Dale brushed himself off, a sudden dizziness coming over him as adrenaline surged through his system. As he steadied himself, he noticed Anna's hood had fallen during the altercation. Over all their years as friends he thought he'd seen every side of Anna. He'd seen her joyful, angry, excited, upset. But this was different. He'd seen her hurt before, he may have been the only one who *had* seen her hurt, but this hurt, the one he'd caused, was different. This was a deep hurt, the sort you can't just recover from, the sort that leaves a scar. Her face was angry, but her eyes told a different story. Dale's brain worked overdrive as he tried to think of words to adequately explain his actions.

"I couldn't come all this way and not see her."

"Is that meant to excuse you? Do you have any idea, *any idea*, how embarrassing that was yesterday? I was standing at that church door just waiting for you. I wanted you there, Dale, I *needed* you there. You're the closest thing I have to family. I thought I could count on you, but you just keep letting me down. You're just as bad as rest of them."

Dale was taken aback, her words hitting like a brick to his heart.

Anna took a few deep breaths, then sat back on the porch. This time, she maintained eye contact. She didn't hide away; she wanted him to know the pain he'd caused.

"When you left New Oxford, when you ran and left *me* behind, that hurt. But I understood that. Things became too much, and typical Dale, you just ran from your problems. I told myself that wasn't personal, it wasn't about me, it was what you needed, and I tried to support you through it. I told myself leaving was hurting you as much as it was me. But it didn't, did it? You didn't give a shit about me then, and you don't now."

"I do care."

"Then why weren't you there yesterday?"

Dale sat on the pavement outside the house. It was cold, uncomfortable, but he had to get off his feet.

"I didn't know what else to do," he started, talking as calmly as he could. "I had a wife, Anna. A wife and a family. And I lost it all. I lost her *twice*. I don't know how to get it back. I don't know how to live without her."

"I know, Dale." Anna's voice had calmed, though she was again avoiding eye contact. "But first, you don't need those things to be happy. You don't need *her* to be happy. Second, if you do want those things, a wife, a family, you can still have that."

3.5: The Distance

"Not with *her*. She's who I'm meant to be with."

Anna crossed her arms and huffed, making her disapproval known.

"I *need* her, Anna."

"And I need you!" A tightness crept back into her voice. "I need you, Dale. Do you know how many people I've *ever* told I loved? Any idea?"

Dale shook his head, the guilt bubbling in his chest.

"Two. My entire life, I've only told two people. You and Bob. And yesterday, with all those people, all that pressure, I needed both of you. I *wanted* both of you. But you treated it like it was nothing."

"I know this wedding was important to you, but—"

"Are you seriously about to *but* me there, Dale?" she snapped. "It's not about the fucking wedding. It's not even about me walking down the aisle to a bunch of sympathetic looks as everyone realised what'd happened. It's about how little stock you put in this friendship. When you talk to me, it's like you're not really present. You're just checking boxes, trying to do *just* enough to keep me ticking over. You're determined to be as distant as you can."

"I moved Anna, I had to."

"I don't mean physically. You have no investment in this anymore. In me. You proved that yesterday."

"I'm sorry, Anna, I'm so sorry. I don't know what else to say."

"What else can be said?"

3.5: The Distance

The two sat silently. Dale kicked his feet against the gravel, something to distract himself. He knew she was right; ever since that holiday he'd been different. How could he not be? She didn't understand what had happened to him anymore than anyone else did. He hadn't yet found the right words to explain how the vision had changed him; he doubted the words existed. But she had, at least, tried to understand it the best she could, and that meant something. He noticed Anna was back to staring at her trainers, her arms crossed, waiting for him to say something.

"So, how was it?" Dale asked casually, attempting to brush off the argument like it was nothing.

"How was what?"

"The wedding. Did everyone have a good time or did Bob's speech put them all to sleep?" he joked, forcing a smile onto his face.

"No!" Anna shouted, once again rising to her feet.

She paced back and forth, her breathing rising with her anger. Dale's misjudged attempt at lightening the mood hung in the air.

She turned to him suddenly, her finger pointing firm. "You don't get to do that anymore. You don't ever, *ever* talk about Bob like that again. Do you understand?"

Dale stood up and tried to move in front of her, hoping to slow her pacing.

"Anna, I was just trying to…"

3.5: The Distance

She stopped a little distance away, staring at him intensely. She brushed the hair away from her face, making sure her eyes were clear.

"We're done, Dale. We're done. Go back to your life, I'll go back to mine. I never want to see you again."

Part 4
The Funeral
15 years after the vision

4.1: The Call

In a portacabin parked inside a fenced-off, dusty building site sat Dale, drowning in paperwork. It was getting late. He should have left more than an hour ago, but with the site crew done for the day this was his best chance to get caught up. The patter of heavy rain on the tin roof helped him think, and it was easier to plan without being disrupted by one of the crew coming to see him every five minutes. Right then, free of distraction, he could focus.

Even with the corners they were cutting, the job was still three months over deadline. They'd be in breach of contract if they didn't get a handle on it soon. Dale had to traverse a fine line between managing the health and safety of the crew and ensuring he didn't cause further delays. Though the site was clear, he still had to wear his high-vis jacket over his tattered hoodie and jeans. He always left his high-vis undone, otherwise his beard, now overgrown and bushy in every direction, would get caught in the zipper.

The form in front of him was a report about one of the temporary contractors who'd had a near-miss fall from the south roof. Usually, it wouldn't have been enough to warrant a report, but she'd been spotted by the site supervisor and upon investigation, it turned out she hadn't been wearing her safety harness. She hadn't been injured but the situation could easily have been much worse. From the thickness of her file, it was clear this wasn't the first time she'd been caught not using her safety equipment properly on a work

4.1: The Call

site. She'd never had an actual accident, but Dale knew the risk was too high – they couldn't afford the delays caused if anything *did* happen. He marked the box titled *not to return to site*.

He moved onto the next incident report. He sighed when he realised it was an M17a: unlicensed forklift use. He'd seen far too many of these this week. He barely had time to read the name before he was distracted by the familiar ringtone of his mobile phone. He grabbed it from his back pocket and stared in disbelief when he saw who it was.

Why would *he* be calling?

"Hello?"

"..."

"Fuck."

"..."

"I'll head down tonight."

Dale hung up the phone, dropped the file onto his desk, then ran through the pouring rain to another cabin just a few feet from his. Inside was the only other member of staff still working: the site manager, Harman, weighed down by as much paperwork as Dale had been moments before. Harman was the only one on the site who wore a smart suit and tie every day. By the time he finished work he'd be covered head to toe in dust, but that didn't stop him; he wanted people to know he was in charge.

"I'm sorry to do this, boss, but I've gotta take off for a couple of days. A week maybe, at most."

"When?"

4.1: The Call

"Now. I've gotta leave tonight. It's a personal matter."

Harman shook his head, equal parts confusion and dismissal. "You can't, Dale. Do you have *any* idea how up against it we are?"

"I know, but I've got no choice. Jenny can cover. I'll be on the phone 24/7 if she needs anything, and I'll catch up with whatever as soon as I'm back."

"No, Dale, the answer is—"

Dale interrupted, "Look, I've not taken a holiday all year. I've been here every night after hours. I know the timing sucks, but I have to go back to New Oxford for a funeral."

Harman stared at his employee and took a moment to think. Dale asking for time off *was* unusual; he knew he wouldn't do it unless it was urgent.

"Alright. I'll get Jenny to call you first thing in the morning, and you can talk her through anything she needs to cover." Harman grabbed a Post-it note from his desk and scribbled something on it before stuffing it into his pocket. "Oh… you were meant to be coming to ours Sunday. Amy was making a curry. Do you think you'll make it?"

"I'm not sure. It depends how long it all takes. Rain check?"

"I'll let her know."

The corner of Dale's mouth lifted almost into a smile. "Tell her the only reason I'm not coming is because my lips are still on fire from last time."

Harman gave a deep belly laugh. "I couldn't taste anything for a week!"

4.1: The Call

Dale quickly dropped back into a feeling of unease, his mind preoccupied with the call. Harman noticed.

"You are alright though, Dale? Do you need anything?"

"I'm fine, don't worry, I've just gotta get home."

"No problem. Just keep me updated on when you're coming back."

"I will. Thanks, boss."

Dale lifted the high-vis over the back of his messy hair, ready to brace the rain again. Just as he was about to step out of the cabin, a thought struck.

"Oh, Harman, you need to call Smith & Andersons. Tell them not to send Mika anymore. Effective immediately."

Harman's eyes bulged in panic. "Are you serious? She's a good worker, Dale. She does three times as much as some of the others from the agency. We can't afford to lose her."

"We can't afford not to. Trust me, just do it... And I know I keep going on about it, but you *must* get those pipes on the second floor changed as a priority. The regulation was updated a week before we started this job. If we get an inspection, they'll close the whole site down."

Dale drove back to his flat, a simple, single-bedroom place in an apartment block less than half an hour from the building site. He rushed in, threw whatever clean clothes he could find from the pile on the floor into a backpack, then got back on the road. The sun was starting to set; the thick clouds and heavy rain made the sky almost black already. It

4.1: The Call

was going to be a gloomy one-hundred-and-sixty-mile journey.

"Shit," he said to himself, shortly after setting off in his car.

He held the steering wheel steady with one hand, then used the other to open the contact list on his phone. He began scrolling down the names, not sure exactly who he was looking for.

"Shit!" he repeated, louder this time. He was struggling to find somebody in the area suitable for what he needed. His eyes continuously flicked between the road and the screen.

"Shit, shit, shit!" He did find somebody… but he knew they wouldn't be happy about it.

He had no choice. He let out a deep sigh, then pressed the call button.

It rang… and rang… and rang. He turned on the loudspeaker, placed the phone down on the passenger seat, then moved his attention fully to the road. Eventually, a soft voice answered.

"Dale?"

"Hello, Emily."

The voice quickly hardened. "You're alive then. What do you want?"

"Could you look after Allo for a few days?"

"Wha… you… is this a joke?" Emily shouted. "Are you actually kidding me right now? I'm… speechless."

"Emily, I—"

4.1: The Call

She was far from speechless. Understandably so.

"Five months, Dale. Five long months I haven't heard so much as a whisper from you. I told you I loved you, and you just ignored me. I came to your apartment, I came to your work, and you just pretended you weren't there. All I got was a half-assed text saying 'it was getting too serious'. Not even an apology! We'd been together almost a year, I don't think that was too early to say the L word. But if it was, or if you didn't feel the same, then you could have just told me. But what you did was cruel. I'm too old for games. You're thirty-seven years old, for goodness' sake. You'll be forty soon. You need to grow up. You're messed up, Dale. You need professional help. You are an emotionally vacant shell of a man. I tried to talk about whatever's wrong with you, but all I got back was 'I can't talk about it'. I gave you space, I did everything a good partner is supposed to do, and what did I get? Not even enough respect to actually dump me. And now, completely out the blue, you call me asking to look after your fucking cat? Are you insane? Are you actually insane? You closed-off, selfish, uncaring—"

"Emily, my mum died."

The phone went silent.

"Emily?"

"Jesus, Dale... I'm so sorry to hear that."

"I know it's a lot to ask, and I know I don't deserve your help—"

"Don't worry," she interrupted. "Of course I'll look after Allo, you know I love that little guy. When do you leave?"

4.1: The Call

"Tonight… I'm heading to New Oxford now. I've just got on the road."

"Okay, bring the key over on your way out of town."

He breathed a sigh of relief. "Thank you."

"But Dale," she said, the harsh tone returning, "I don't want to see you, okay? Just drop the key through the letterbox."

"I understand."

4.2: The Home

How long had it been since Dale had been back there?

There was the odd family event, not that he'd attended many of them. Often he'd had – or more realistically, often he'd *found* – some convenient excuse for not making the journey back. Occasionally he did make the effort, though that had been fewer times in the last decade than he could count on both hands. He kept in contact with his mother, texted her once every couple of weeks to check in, but actually going to New Oxford was just too painful. Whenever he did return, he tended to stay at the Sleep'n'save a couple of miles away.

How long had it been since he'd stayed a night in his old family home?

He couldn't even remember.

The house changed a lot after Jak's accident. The dining room was converted into his bedroom, all the door frames were widened so he could get through them and a chairlift had been installed over the staircase. That was almost twenty years ago now, yet Dale somehow always forgot about the changes. Or maybe forgot wasn't the right word. It was just that most of his memories of his home were split into two categories: what it was like in his *other* life, and what it was like in this one. In the other life, Jak died in the accident, so the house had never been converted. In this one, Dale moved out shortly after the changes were made, so they didn't exist for most of the time he lived there.

4.2: The Home

Even though he hadn't stayed there in such a long time, he still kept a key. Standing inside, alone, it hit him just how empty the house felt without his mother there.

He dropped his rucksack in the spare room. It was once his old bedroom, but now it was empty save for a single bed and an old wardrobe. Dale stripped it shortly after he left home. He'd assumed his mum and Jak would do something with it, turn it into a home office or a games room or whatever, but they never did. Still, even void of his identity, being back there created an unusual feeling for Dale. It was a mix of comfort and unease.

Dale awoke to the sound of the front door opening downstairs, the blazing sunshine flooding through the window catching him off guard. He hadn't realised he'd fallen asleep; he didn't even remember lying down. Was it really morning already? The curtains were open, and he was still wearing his clothes from the previous day. He must have passed out, exhausted from the drive.

"Dale?" Jak shouted. "You here?"

Dale rubbed the sleep from his eyes. He slowly shuffled out the door and to the top of the stairs.

"I'm up here."

He saw Jak waiting at the bottom of the staircase, wearing black trousers and a smart lemon polo shirt – he was dressed much smarter than Dale. He always was. Anna used to say that what Jak lacked in mobility, he made up for in style. His short hair was immaculately combed, his goatee perfectly trimmed; every hair purposefully positioned. He was

4.2: The Home

three years older yet looked more youthful than Dale. He was sitting in his wheelchair, looking up to catch a glimpse of his brother.

Dale, in comparison, looked a bit of a mess. They both knew it.

"When did you get here?" Jak asked, as Dale walked down the stairs towards him, using the banister to steady himself – he wasn't fully with it yet.

"Last night. It was pretty late. Where were you?"

"At home. You should've said, I would have come over."

Dale reached the bottom of the stairs. He frowned as he attempted to process what his brother had said.

"Home? You don't live here?"

Jak scowled at his brother. "What are you talking about? I moved out over ten years ago."

"Well, you were always here when I came home."

"Yeah, because, Dale, on those rare occasions you *actually* came home, I'd always be here to see you."

"Oh... fair enough then."

There was a moment of silence between the two, neither sure what to say. Dale felt more uncomfortable every minute he was there, but he was pushing through it. His brother had specifically asked him to stay at the old house on this occasion. Given that Jak had dealt with all the funeral plans, Dale thought it only fair that he did as he asked.

Jak sensed his brother's unease and broke the tension the only way he knew how. "Shall I put the kettle on then?"

4.2: The Home

The kitchen windowsill was cluttered with photo frames containing old family pictures. Dale scanned them. There was Jak at his university graduation – even with the gown stuck in the spoke of his wheels he still looked *cool*. Next was Dale and Anna from their school prom – his eyes lingered on that one for a moment, and he chuckled to himself thinking back to that night. The two got all dressed up, then spent the evening sitting in the corner guessing what everyone else there would be doing in ten years, pushing each other to see who could come up with the bleakest story. His eyes moved to the next picture – his mother on the beach in her bikini with two young boys in front of her. The picture had been folded over, cutting someone off on the other side. Dale picked it up for a closer look at the boys; he couldn't remember ever being that young. He looked even closer at his mum; she looked so joyful, so free.

"Feels weird without her here, doesn't it?" Jak said. He wheeled over to the kitchen table with a tray on his lap. One by one, he lifted the mugs from the tray and placed them on the table.

Dale put the picture down and sat opposite his brother. He took a sip of the coffee; the bitterness pulled him right back to old memories. His mum had bought the same coffee her whole life. It was cheap and nasty, and Dale dreaded it whenever he visited. He and Heather, in the *other* life, once brought their own over instead. Margaret took great offence to it – they never made that mistake again. But now, with the piping hot mug in front of him smelling like musty tar, he couldn't wait to taste it again.

4.2: The Home

"Were you with her?" Dale asked. "At the end, I mean."

"Not at the *very* end, no. But I was there for most of the time she was at the hospital."

"Right."

Right. No 'good', no 'thank you Jak for being there', but he expected no more from his brother.

"What time's the funeral tomorrow?"

"Eleven. You know, she actually helped arrange most of it."

"Who did?"

"Mum," Jak said. "She knew she only had a few days left, that's why it's happened so quickly. She knew what she wanted and she didn't want it all falling on us. Well... falling on me." He couldn't help himself.

Dale brushed it off. "Will... is Noah coming?" he asked sheepishly.

"I haven't told him. I don't even have his number."

"Good."

Noah was their father, though neither called him that. He'd held some sort of resentment towards both the boys ever since they were born. He wasn't built to be a father; he hated having any sort of responsibility. Dale was twenty when Noah left out the blue one day. No note, no goodbye. All of them – Jak, Dale and even their mother, though she never said it – were grateful that he was gone. It was like a weight had been lifted. Jak blamed himself for a while, that the accident put even more responsibility on an already-struggling Noah. But Dale assured him that Noah had

4.2: The Home

abandoned them in the vision too; it was just who he was. Jak wasn't sure if he believed him, but he took some comfort in it anyway.

"So, how are you, brother?" Jak reluctantly sipped the bitter coffee. "How's life outside of New Oxford?"

"Yeah, fine. Busy." Dale watched as Jak smirked; he was clearly trying to start up a conversation. "It's weird being back. There's a *lot* of memories here. It's like stepping back into an old life."

"Speaking of," Jak casually tried to bring the conversation around to something he'd wanted to say, "you should really go and see her."

Dale rubbed his face with both hands. "Trust me, I've thought of nothing else since I got back. Actually..." Dale wasn't sure why he was about to be so open. It wasn't like him to talk to Jak about his thoughts, or about anything, really. But being back home, especially under the circumstances, was making him feel... different. "Even when I'm away, she's still in the back of my mind. There are many, *many* nights I've had to resist driving back and going to see her."

"Well, what's stopping you? She's still in the same house, and I know she'd love to hear from you."

"I'm not so sure. On both counts. I heard she's got married again."

"Again?" Jak frowned. "She's only been married once, Dale."

"You know what I mean." Dale shifted back to the windowsill of memories, as his mind thought back to his

4.2: The Home

other life. There used to be pictures of Heather in the hospital with baby Lynn in her arms, Aiden on his first day of school, Dale at work with both kids on his knees. That windowsill was once full of pictures of his mother's grandkids, but she'd never got to meet them here.

Jak shook his head. He'd seen Dale avoid meeting his eye many times since that boat trip. "Dale, who do you think I'm talking about?"

"Heather. My wife. Well, you know what I mean."

"Anna!" Jak threw his arms in the air, as if trying to get through to his brother. "I'm talking about Anna. You should reach out to Anna."

"Oh… yeah, maybe." Dale dismissed it.

"She sent a lovely card, by the way." Jak signalled to the plethora of condolence cards on the mantelpiece in the other room. "I wasn't sure if I should invite her and Bob…"

Jak noticed Dale was still staring at the pictures. He clicked his fingers a few times to try to get his attention.

"Dale, you there?"

"Yeah, sorry." He turned back to his brother.

"Well, look," Jak said, placing his empty mug down on the table. "I've got some final details to sort for the funeral. It'd be nice to have some help, brothers back together again, what do you think?"

"I, uh." Dale wasn't sure he had the energy in him. "I was planning to just hang out here, maybe take a walk into the old town or something."

4.2: The Home

"It would be good if it wasn't *all* left to me. She was your mother too, Dale."

He was right. Dale had assumed Jak would just take care of it all – or at least, just that someone else would do it.

"Fine. Give me a list of stuff and I'll get it done."

"Or we could do it together?"

"Just get me a list." Dale ignored Jak's attempts to spend time together. "It'll be easier that way."

4.3: The Reception

Gathered in the church were a collection of Margaret's closest friends, a handful of family, and a few of her ex-work colleagues from back before she retired. This particular church was chosen as it contained their family plot, where Margaret's mother and father were already buried. Her two sons stood inside the doorway, Jak looking immaculate in a simple but somehow-still-stylish black suit, and Dale in a pinstripe suit that was several sizes too small. The two greeted the guests as they arrived. Each one Dale would assume to be the last, yet they kept coming. He barely recognised a face in there, but Jak seemed to know them all.

"I'm sorry for your loss."

"She was a wonderful woman."

"She loved you both."

The same phrases on repeat. They quickly grew tiresome, but Dale knew people were just trying to share comfort the only way they knew how. Dale could see behind Jak's smile that the morning was getting to him, that the reality of losing his mother was hitting hard. Dale knew he should be feeling more, or at least feeling *something*, but he was just… blank. This wasn't the first time he'd buried his mother; he remembered having to explain to Aiden and Lynn that their grandmother had passed. She was their first grandparent to go, and the first time they'd experienced death. Navigating them through it felt impossible at the time, but not for Heather. She knew exactly what to say. She

4.3: The Reception

likened it to a star. "We look up and see the diamonds in the sky, and yet many of them have already died. We only see them because their light continues its journey. We see the star clear and real; to us it is as alive as anything else in life." She told them that memories are a person's light continuing to shine. As long as we remember them, they'll stay as alive as the stars.

Dale was suddenly pulled back to reality when he felt a hand grab his.

"She will be missed," an elderly man said as he took hold of Dale's hand.

Dale pulled it away and stormed out of the church.

"Excuse him," Jak said politely. "It's a difficult day."

As soon as the guest passed by, Jak followed his brother, wheeling after him as fast as he could.

"Dale!" Jak shouted. "Wait a minute."

Dale stopped at the end of the pathway, just short of the gate that led out of the church grounds. "I need to go. I need to see her."

"See who?"

"Heather. She should be here, she loved Mum."

"What are you talking about? She didn't know her."

Dale's jaw tensed and his voice sharpened. "Yes, she did! She knew her for decades. She loved her like a second mother. I need to see her, Jak, I need to see her."

"Really, Dale? You have to do this *today*?" Jak scoffed and began heading back towards the church. "Can't we have

4.3: The Reception

one day together without you talking about that bloody dream?"

"It wasn't a dream!" Dale shouted, louder than his brother, loud enough for the church to hear.

"Fine," Jak spun his chair back around. "Call it whatever you want. But right now, we need to bury our mother, and I'm finding that hard enough to deal with without this. Don't make this day about you. It's about *her*. Show her some respect."

The words bounced around in his head. Jak was right. Heather had attended the funeral once before; the people here never had. This day was for them. Dale nodded, then silently joined his brother, the two doing their best to ignore the staring crowd as they headed back into the church.

The reception was held at a pub across the road from the church, the Red Lion. They closed it to regular customers for the afternoon. Dale arrived later than the rest. He told them he had to take a work call before heading in, but really he just needed a moment to himself. The funeral had been a relatively composed affair. Jak read a passage from her favourite book, something Dale had never even heard of. He felt guilty for that, but thankfully the feeling didn't last long. The priest said what little comforting words he could about "a better place" and "finding peace". They played *Daylight & Dreaming* by *Faith Haart*, her favourite song, as the coffin was taken to be buried. For Jak, he was surrounded by loved ones. But for Dale, most of them were strangers.

4.3: The Reception

He took a few minutes outside the pub to stretch his muscles and enjoy the cold air. He was pre-tired, knowing he was going to have to expend some social energy that evening. He sighed, closed his eyes, then walked through the door.

The place was darkly lit, with a number of empty pool tables pushed aside to make room for the buffet table. There were people everywhere Dale looked; it seemed like more than had been in the church, but given they were all dressed in black, he assumed it was the smaller space making their numbers appear larger. There was a low, consistent mumbling of overlapping conversations, slightly louder than Dale would like. Much of it seemed to be coming from the bar area, where mourners had gathered to try to get a drink and ended up in conversation. Dale didn't have the energy to stand with them. He looked around for a quiet place he could retreat to.

"Dale!" Jak shouted enthusiastically.

Dale sighed, realising he wasn't going to be able to hide away. He spotted Jak in the corner of the pub, away from most of the others. He was at a round table with three other people, none of whom Dale recognised. All were in their early forties, the same age as Jak. Not that Dale was far off that himself. Jak ushered Dale over to the table, an empty chair with a pint already waiting.

"Hi," Dale said awkwardly as he reached them. He didn't want to assume the empty chair was for him; he'd hoped it wasn't.

"Sit down," Jak insisted.

4.3: The Reception

Dammit.

The table was far too small for five of them, but no one seemed to mind. There was a stray chair to one side – Dale realised they must have pushed it away so that Jak could get his in.

"This is my mate, Grame." Jak signalled to the heavyset, balding man with a big bushy beard sitting next to his brother. The two shook hands.

"How ya doin'?" Grame said in a thick Scottish accent.

Dale nodded, then moved his attention to the next person around the table, a woman with long jet-black hair. As she turned to Dale, he noticed a large tattoo of a red rose on the side of her neck.

"This is Misa," Jak said, continuing the introductions. "She's my... umm... she's a..."

He awkwardly searched for the right words to define what they were. Luckily, she stopped him from having to find them (only after joyfully watching him squirm).

"Hi Dale, Jak has told us all about you." She reached across the table and shook his hand.

Jak moved to the last person at the table. "And obviously, you know Carly."

"Hey, long time no see," she said casually, as if they'd spoken a hundred times before.

"Hey, how you doing?" Dale searched her face to try to place her. There was nothing, not even a flicker of recognition. Dale thought that her large facial features and

4.3: The Reception

blonde bob gave her a striking look, not one you'd quickly forget, and yet he could swear he'd never seen her before.

"You have no idea who I am, do you?" Carly laughed. Dale obviously hadn't been subtle enough.

Jak grinned as he peered around to his brother, finding his lack of recognition as amusing as Carly did.

"I'm Joyce's daughter."

The penny dropped. "Oh! Cousin Carly!" Dale exclaimed. "I haven't seen you since we were, what, nine?"

"Something like that."

"So yer the brother with the psychic ability, are ya?" Grame said abruptly across the table. Jak winced, throwing his friend a look as if to say *that's a sore subject*.

"Uh, what?" Dale was caught off guard.

"Oh aye, Jak said you saw the future or something? You've no' got this week's Powerball numbers, have ya?" Grame joked, smiling from cheek to cheek. It was clear he meant no malice in asking; it was probably the only thing he knew about Dale, and he was trying to make conversation. Dale smiled politely and brushed it off all the same.

Jak took Dale's reluctance to respond as a sign that he needed to cut in. He raised his pint of beer high into the air.

"To Mum," he shouted. "The kindest, funniest, and most generous woman I've ever known. When she died, the universe lost a tiny part of itself, but to some of us, we lost a large part of our universe. Please, join me in toasting the woman who taught me everything I know."

4.3: The Reception

The whole group raised their glasses and knocked them together, with a collective "To Margaret".

Carly placed a comforting hand on Jak, smiling sweetly. She'd noticed that he was holding something back, not wanting to share any further emotion in that moment.

"Well, baws," Grame said, "I'll never get that £50 now she's dead."

Dale was taken aback. He felt the hairs on the back of his neck rise, almost in protest at someone being so callous about his mother just after she'd died. Around him, the mood of the table lifted as the others erupted into laughter.

"Oh give over!" Misa shouted, as joyful as Grame was. "She didn't owe you anything!"

"Look," Grame continued, "we all ken she did. And I 'hink the only reason she died was so she didnae have ta pay me."

The sounds of friendly laughter filled the air once again.

"Well, you're not getting it from me!" Jak joked.

"What's this?" Dale whispered to Jak, but not as quietly as planned.

It was Cousin Carly who answered. "We have this sort of semi-regular poker night. It's meant to be for fun, but *some* people" — she playfully glared at Grame and Misa, her head shifting between the two – "take it *far* too seriously! Anyway, Aunty Margaret used to join us sometimes, and, what was it, a week ago?"

Jak nodded.

4.3: The Reception

Carly continued, "We held it at the hospital, so she could be a part of it. The first couple of hands were a warm up, and your mum, being the badass that she was, went all-in on the second hand! She bet everything she had in her purse. Grame called her; she was sitting on three jacks, he had four aces."

"It wisnae a warm up!" Grame shouted playfully. "The first game is a warm up, no' the first few. Always been that way."

"Give over," Misa said. "You're just a sore loser!"

"Speaking of sore losers..." Jak signalled to his brother. "Dale used to be the worst for that!"

"What are you talking about?" Dale said, scrunching his eyebrows. It wasn't what Jak had said, it was the fact he was being brought into the conversation.

"Back when we were teenagers" – Jak moved his attention back to the whole table – "we used to have this thing, right, where we'd argue over whose turn it was to wash up. So, we'd play for it. One round on *Street Fighter*, the loser had to do the chores. Every time Dale lost, which was *most* of the time, he'd slam the controller down and shout."

Dale's mind wandered back to a time he hadn't thought about in years. "Only because you used to spam the same move over and over again."

"A win's a win, Dale! You were a sore loser, and you know it. You'd get so angry! You'd go screaming to Mum about how I cheated."

"What would she do?" Carly asked.

4.3: The Reception

"She told me to get the chores done, and that the next time Jak went out she'd help me practise."

"That's so Aunty Margaret!" Carly said.

"That woman was a queen," Misa added.

Dale had never thought of his mum like that. He'd never thought of her much beyond being his mother.

Misa started laughing to herself. "Do you remember that time she came over and let herself into yours?"

Jak's face turned a bright shade of pink. "Please don't!"

"Now you've gotta tell us!" Grame shouted. Loud seemed to be his default.

"Right." Misa rubbed her hands together, excited to get into the story. "Do you remember when Jak had that thing at the office where he couldn't go into work?"

"The asbestos," Jak said reluctantly.

Dale didn't know his brother worked in an office. He didn't even know he worked at all.

"Yeah, that thing," Misa said. "Anyway, I get this text. Jak tells me he's gotta go home, and if I've got nothing to do then *why don't I come over for a coffee – or something, winky face*."

"So smooth, Jak," Carly joked.

Misa continued, "We're, you know, on his sofa, things are getting going, our clothes are all over the place. But then we realise we haven't got a condom. So I head off to the bathroom…"

4.3: The Reception

Dale sat back in disbelief at how openly she was talking, and how normal it was to them all. He had no idea that Jak had such a close group of friends.

"I'm searching through the cupboards when I hear his front door open. It's Margaret. Jak forgot that he'd asked her to drop off the paperwork for his mortgage application."

"Ach no!" Grame laughed.

"Suddenly, I hear this thump in the other room, and Jak shouting."

All eyes turned to Jak, who was playfully shaking his head, his cheeks flourishing even brighter. "Did we have to tell this story?"

"Too late now," Misa replied, winking.

Jak picked up the story. "Mum walked in to find me stark bollock-naked on the sofa. In a panic, I rolled over to grab my chair, but we'd been in such a rush to get onto the sofa that we hadn't put the brakes on. So the chair went flying, and I fell bang on the floor, panicking like a turtle stuck on its back!"

"Where were you?" Carly asked Misa.

"Still in the bathroom! I didn't have anything on either. No way I was leaving."

"Mum lifted me up onto the sofa," Jak continued, "she threw the clothes from the floor onto me, moved my chair back, put the brakes on, chucked the papers on the table, then left."

4.3: The Reception

Misa jumped in, "On the way out she shouted, 'Good morning, Misa' through the bathroom door, to which I sheepishly said, 'Uh, hi... sorry, Mrs Sawyer.'"

The sound of laughter was deafening, and only grew louder as the stories continued.

People regularly came over to the table to pay their respects over the course of the afternoon. Each had their own amusing anecdote about Margaret, Jak, or both. Dale listened, his mind unable to fully process what he was hearing. These stories about his mother and his brother may as well have been about strangers – these were not the people he knew. He was starting to feel like an outsider at his own mother's funeral.

Between each story, the pints kept flowing, and the group kept laughing. Dale hadn't involved himself in the conversation much; he felt like a fly on the wall, looking into a life he didn't know his brother had. As the evening drew in, and more people left, it didn't take long for the place to feel empty. Not that it slowed the group down – they barely even noticed people leaving. But Dale found he could see much more of the pub than before, and something about the place wasn't sitting right. Something was triggering a memory deep in his mind, but it was too quick, too fuzzy, to grab hold. How did he know this pub? Was it the decor? The tables? The bar? The bar... he'd stood at *that* bar before, a *long* time ago... he was in a pinstripe suit then, too. It was another funeral.

Suddenly, it hit him.

4.3: The Reception

He excused himself from the banter and left as quickly as he could, bursting through the door to catch his breath. His chest was tight, his muscles tense, a metallic taste in his mouth. How had he not noticed where they were? He was so focused on breathing that he didn't hear the door open behind him.

"You alright, bro?" Jak said, slurring his words. "You look like you've seen a ghost."

"I'm fine. It doesn't matter." Dale paced back and forth furiously.

"Come on, what's going on?" Jak did his best impression of a serious face, while focusing on not spilling what little was left in his glass.

"This pub – the Red Lion – this is where I met Heather. It's where we came after your funeral."

"Wow." Jak's head wobbled, mostly from alcohol, but partly from trying to process what was said. "Well, that's fucked up. Why would you tell me that?"

"You asked."

"Fair enough… So you coming back in, or what?" Jak's eyes were barely able to focus.

Dale's pacing increased. He didn't have the energy to go back in there. He didn't have the energy to pretend to be okay.

"I'm just gonna go home, I think."

"Oh come on, the night is young." Jak downed what was left of his drink.

"I'm not in the mood."

4.3: The Reception

"You can't just get a cob on every time you're reminded of your imaginary life. This is the second time today I've had to chase after you."

"You know what, Jak?" Dale stopped in his tracks, a firm finger pointing towards his brother. "Fuck you! You have no idea what I went through."

"Oh boohoo, Dale. It's always the victim with you," Jak spat, his head unsteady from the alcohol.

"I lost my kids!" Dale screamed.

"No, you imagined you had kids. That's not the same thing."

Dale's eyes filled with fury. "You don't know what it's like. You don't know what *real* loss is."

"I don't know what loss is? Really, Dale? You talk about what you lost from that *thing*, but what about what you gained?"

"Gained? What exactly did I gain, Jak?"

"*Me!*" Jak shouted, his voice tense and pained. "You gained me. In your dream, or *vision*, or whatever you want to call it, I was dead, right? But I'm not dead here. You're my brother, that really means something to me, but it means *nothing* to you. You say I don't know what loss is, but do you know what I lost when you went on that holiday? I lost you!" He took a breath and allowed the tension to release, just a little. "I lost my brother. The Dale I knew never came back from Greece."

"I'm right here."

4.3: The Reception

"You've never been the same, Dale. We used to be close, you and I. Even after the accident, when everyone treated me differently, you never did. But then you went on holiday, and ever since then you won't even look at me."

Dale stopped still and stared at his brother.

"I'm looking at you now, Jak."

"Not really… you're looking *through* me." Jak did his best to focus, but his eyes were heavy, his blinks lasting longer than they should. His mind, however, was clear. He knew what he wanted to say. "I hear it in your voice every time you talk to me. Sometimes, I sense you staring at me when I'm looking the other way. But when I turn around, you rush away, because you know, *you know*, that if our eyes meet it would give away the truth."

"What truth?"

Jak savoured the icy air – like his brother, it helped him think. It helped him build the courage to say something he'd suppressed for years. "That I killed your children."

The words lingered uncomfortably around them. The bitter air somehow felt colder. Dale found himself unable to speak, unable to move.

"That day," Jak said, calmer than before, "when you came home from Greece, without Suzanne, and you told us what happened… that hurt. It hurt more than the accident ever did. I heard it in every word you said, the truth of how you felt… That in this life, your family had been traded for *me*. It was all over your face. Do you have any idea what that's like? Being in this chair, being a burden to this family, I thought that was the guilt I was going to have to carry

4.3: The Reception

forever. But *this*" – he gestured to his chair – "is *nothing* compared to the guilt you make me feel every time we speak."

"I have never once said that, Jak."

"You don't have to. You scream it without ever saying it. My literal existence prevented theirs. That's the truth, Dale. And we need to stop skirting around it and just face it. Because I can't keep going on like this with you. Every time you come back here, I just feel like shit."

Dale caught himself as his knees buckled, lowering down to the pavement. His thoughts were fast, overlapping, and uncomfortable, like a beehive stuck in his skull. He wanted to talk, but his vocal cords were too numb to let out a sound.

"I'm sorry for what happened to you, Dale. But you need to face this and move on."

Jak wheeled himself over to be next to his brother. Dale's head was dipped, staring at the floor, numb. Jak went to place his hand on his shoulder but lost the nerve just before it made contact.

"Back in there, when we were talking about *Street Fighter*," Jak said, "it reminded me of how angry you used to get. How happy. How upset. But this, how you are now… it's like you've died." He found the courage to give him a comforting touch. He squeezed his brother's shoulder, hoping to get through to him. "I *really* think you need to call her. Your life has fallen off course without her. You need her, Dale."

4.3: The Reception

"I know. You're right, Jak. I do need her. We saw what we saw because we are *meant* to be together."

Jak removed his hand as his voice raised once again.

"Anna! For fuck's sake, Dale! You need to talk to Anna."

Dale allowed Anna to come to the forefront of his mind. The truth was, he did miss her. Maybe Jak was right, maybe he did need her back in his life. But what life did he have without Heather? She *was* his life.

"I need Heather, Jak." Dale lifted his head, as if he suddenly had something to focus on, a clear vision. "I need my wife."

Jak rolled his eyes. "She isn't your wife. She never was your wife. She will never *be* your wife. I'm sorry, brother, I know it sucks, but I think the only way to get past it is to accept it."

"No offence, Jak" – Dale found the energy to rise up and brush himself off – "but you have *no* idea what you're talking about."

Jak scoffed and laughed sarcastically. Just as he was about to reply, the door opened behind them.

"Are you guys okay? We heard shouting," Misa asked delicately as she came outside.

"We're fine." Jak looked over his shoulder to her. "We're coming back in now. Come on, Dale. Let's forget all this and go have fu-" Jak turned back to realise Dale was already too far away to hear. His shoulders dropped as the disappointment hit. Misa reached from behind him and wrapped her arms around him, pulling herself in tight to the

4.3: The Reception

back of his chair and resting her arms on his chest. It was a comforting embrace.

4.4: The Name

Dale was alone in the kitchen of his old family home, struggling to keep his eyes open as he stared into his bowl of cereal. The events of the previous evening had kept him awake, but he was no stranger to a sleepless night. He'd planned to stay there for a few days, but now he wasn't sure Jak wanted him to. He wasn't sure *he* wanted to. What was he staying for? He kept replaying their conversation in his head. Had Jak been right? Of course he had, of course Dale had changed after that holiday, how could he not have? He had more memories of his other life than he did this one.

"Morning," Jak said as he wheeled himself into the kitchen. He pulled open the blinds with an enthusiasm far greater than he should have for someone who'd drunk as much as he had the night before. Dale squinted as the room filled with golden sunlight. He grumbled, making his disapproval known.

"Coffee?" Jak asked, grabbing the kettle. The kitchen sides were low enough for Jak to grab whatever he needed; their mother had designed them that way. She'd worked hard to ensure Jak kept as much independence as possible after the accident.

"Oi, Dale," he said playfully, "do you want a coffee or not?"

Dale grunted dismissively, not once looking up from his breakfast.

4.4: The Name

"Ah, this brings back memories!" Jak grabbed a mug and put one... two... no, today was a two and a half spoons of coffee day, into the mug. "It's a beautiful morning, and here you are silently sulking into your Coco Pops."

Dale tossed his unfinished bowl aside and got to his feet, ready to leave the room.

"Oh, sit down, you grumpy bastard! I'm just messing."

"I've got stuff to do," Dale lied.

"No, you haven't." Jak grabbed a second mug from the side. "Just sit and have a coffee with me. You're not leaving me alone to sort all of Mum's estate."

Shit. Dale hadn't considered the estate. He thought he would be back for the funeral and that was it. He sighed and sat back down, bracing himself for the incoming tedium of decision-making and paperwork.

Jak finished making coffee, then wheeled both mugs over to the table. He slid one over to his brother, unsure if he would take it.

"The business is sorted. She said she asked you if you wanted to run it?" Jak said.

"Yeah, she did. I said no, I did that for long enough in... you know."

"Fine, I don't want it either. She's left it to Saanvi. She became the manager after Mum got sick. But you and I still have shares just in case Saanvi ever decides to sell up."

Dale shrugged.

"But," Jak continued, "we do need to sort this house. I've got an estate agent coming later today to price it up.

4.4: The Name

Apparently, because it's designed around wheelchair access, it'll be a fairly easy sell. There's some specialist places where they can list it. Still, we need to get that sorted, and then deal with the money. It's in both our names now, so—"

"If you deal with it, you can have *all* of it," Dale interrupted without thinking.

"You can't be serious? Dale, there's no mortgage on this. It needs some work, sure, but a three-bedroom house in this neighbourhood has gotta be, what, 200k at least?"

"I am serious," Dale said, and he was. "I'd rather not have the headache. You can have my share."

Jak rubbed his eyes. "I'm not taking your money, Dale. But don't worry, I'll sort the house."

Dale started to shuffle in his seat again, desperate to get up and leave the room. Jak could see how uncomfortable he was. He closed his eyes and sighed.

"I've got something for you," Jak said slowly. "But I *really* don't think you should use it."

Dale looked at his brother sideways, confused, trying to work out what he was talking about. Jak reached into his pocket, then slid a piece of paper slowly across the table.

"What is…" Dale unfolded it to reveal a phone number.

"It's Heather's." Jak's voice was filled with hesitation.

Dale's eyes fixed on the paper in disbelief. "You two know each other?"

"No, not at all, actually," Jak said. "But we have… overlapping circles."

4.4: The Name

Dale ran his hand through his hair, trying to process it.

"Why are you giving this to me?"

Jak wasn't entirely sure how to answer that. He wasn't really sure why he was doing it... It didn't feel right giving it to his brother, but he knew Dale was stuck. It had been so long since that holiday, *so* long, and yet Dale still seemed as lost as the day he got back. This was the only thing Jak could think to do. For better or worse, at least it would be different – or so he hoped.

"Look, I don't think you should call her. But you need to do *something*. And you know what you need more than I do, I think."

Dale didn't even give it a second thought. He grabbed the paper tightly in his hand and rushed out of the room.

The park was quieter than expected. There was a chill in the air, sure, but the sun was shining enough that Dale thought it would bring families out, yet the place was almost empty. Dale sat on a bench and watched a kid, no older than three or four, being pushed on a swing by his father. They were the only other people in the park. Watching them was peaceful, though Dale could feel his nerves rising with each passing moment.

"Hi Dale."

Her voice caused all the tension to leave his body, the air to leave his lungs, and a warmth to engulf every part of his skin. Meeting in the park had been her idea. She'd said on the phone that she wanted some fresh air, but Dale suspected she wanted to meet in public.

4.4: The Name

"Heather," he said, his face lighting up as she walked around the bench, though he tried not to let it show. She looked so different from the last time he saw her. Her hair was still a flourish of dark curls, but her face carried with it a tiredness that was more than just her age. In fact, she must be forty now, or close to, and he remembered how youthful she looked at that age in their other life. Here, it was different, and Dale knew why. He saw it in his own face every day – what'd happened had given them a heavy weight to carry.

Dale presented his arms for a hug, then quickly dropped them and extended his hand. He chuckled to himself. "We've been here before, haven't we? Do we hug, kiss, bow?"

"I think let's just sit," she said, her expression more serious than Dale's. More nervous.

Her hands remained firmly planted in the pockets of her denim jacket. She only removed them for a moment to straighten her skirt over her leggings as she sat, then they quickly returned to the pockets. It was clear she was uncomfortable.

"You look well." Dale smiled in her direction, happy she was sitting so close to him.

"You do, too," she said softly. She was perched on the edge of the bench, like a coiled spring ready to bounce up and leave at a moment's notice.

"I heard you're married now." The words caught his throat as they left; his attempt at being nonchalant had failed. "Congratulations. Steve, was it? Or Shane?"

4.4: The Name

"Umm, Eric." She started fiddling with her wedding ring, visibly uncomfortable. "I... I have a son, too. From a previous relationship."

"Oh." Dale swallowed. That'd taken him by surprise, but he was trying to stay positive. "What, um... how old is he?"

"He's eight. He's at school today. I've gotta pick him up later."

"Well, I'm happy for you," Dale lied, flatly. "So what's his name?"

"What about you, Dale? How are you?"

It was clear that Heather didn't want to discuss her personal life with him.

"Yeah, you know. Work is busy, it uh, it drives me mad, but actually I think I like it. Being busy stops me from thinking, you know?"

Heather nodded. She really did know.

"Plus, I think this might actually be something I'm good at. I don't dread going to work every day. That's a win, I think." Dale smiled, mostly to himself, at how easy it felt to talk to her. He'd barely said two words about his job to anybody else, but he felt like he wanted to tell her everything. He resisted the urge to say more, for now.

"That's good," she said, with a kind smile, a smile he'd missed seeing.

"Oh, it was Mum's funeral yesterday."

"I'm so sorry." Heather removed her hand from her pocket and took hold of his. "I'd heard she'd passed. I thought about making contact, but I just wasn't sure it was a good idea."

"I know what you mean... What about you, Heather? You're a big-shot author now, that must be exciting."

She sniggered to herself. "I was, once upon a time. Not sure I am anymore. I don't know if you heard, but my last book didn't exactly do so well."

"Those critics don't know what they're talking about! I don't think they really understood it."

"You read it? *Fire in Chains*?"

"I've read everything you've written."

Heather wasn't sure how to react. It was nice that he'd followed her career, yet for some reason it made her feel uneasy. Exposed.

"The critics *were* right," she said. "When I talked about *us*, I had a lot to say. I had things I needed to get out of me. There was a point, even if I didn't understand what that was. But with nothing left I just started writing for the sake of writing. It didn't have the same punch."

"Well, I liked it a lot more than the stuff you wrote about us."

Dale's admission killed the conversation, but her hand was still on his, their fingers now interlocked. They looked out at the park, watching the kid still on the swing, smelling the freshly cut grass, feeling the breeze, listening to the sound of the birds; it was so peaceful. Dale took a moment to savour it – the two of them together, not fighting, it was

4.4: The Name

just... everything. He didn't want to blink for fear he'd lose some of it.

The father they were watching stopped the swing and walked his kid over to the climbing frame, a mesh of flaking red painted metal. The kid quickly climbed from one beam to the next, the father contorting under each, ready to catch him if he fell.

"Wait," Dale said, his mouth lifting to a smile. "Isn't that where Lynn broke her finger?"

Heather removed her hand from his and used it to block the sun from her eyes. She carefully surveyed the climbing frame.

"Wow, I think you're right. It is! I forgot all about that."

"She was so happy with herself that she'd climbed to the top," Dale recalled, "then *bang!* She tumbled like a sack of spuds."

"I don't think I'd ever seen you move so fast. I heard you shouting before I'd properly registered what'd happened."

"I think I scared Lynn more than the fall," Dale said. "She found the whole thing hilarious."

Heather winced. "I remember you carrying her over, her finger bent the wrong way, and she had the biggest smile on her face. She didn't even react to the pain, she just kept yelling, 'Did you see me mummy? I got to the top!'"

"That was so Lynn."

The two allowed themselves a moment to think back. Think sideways? Being there together, even through the

4.4: The Name

awkwardness, was a comfort to them both – like they'd been wearing a suit all day, but now they were home and in pyjamas.

"Oh," Heather said laughing, "guess who I saw the other day?"

"Who?"

"Jane... As in Aiden's girlfriend, Jane."

"No way," Dale said, in genuine shock. He hadn't thought about Jane in so long. "What did you say to her?"

"Nothing. What could I say? She was just a teenager. It was so odd to see her like that. Can you imagine how weird it would have been to try and explain it to her?"

"Wow... I do *not* miss Jane," Dale joked.

The silence returned, but it wasn't an uncomfortable one. It was nice, calm, tranquil.

"Heather, do you..." Dale swallowed. "Do you still think about them?"

She pulled the sleeve of her jacket over her fingers and used it to wipe a tear.

"Every day."

"Do you ever think about me?"

Heather paused. She turned and looked him in the eye.

"*Every* day. I'm glad you called, Dale."

"Me too. I miss you so much, Heather. Nobody understands what it's like."

4.4: The Name

"I don't think they ever will," she replied, her tone loaded with similar experiences of failed attempts at explaining what they went through.

"When did life become so complicated? One minute I was sneaking across the hallway in the middle of the night because, even though you were nineteen, your mum wouldn't let us stay in the same room together. The next everything became so... heavy."

"I know."

Heather stood up off the bench and extended her arm towards Dale.

"Come on," she said, pulling him to his feet, "let's go for a walk."

The two slowly wandered out of the park and through the street. This was one of the quieter parts of New Oxford. There was a post office, a couple of cafes, the occasional newsagents, not that either of them paid much attention to their surroundings. They were too busy chatting like old friends.

No - old family.

"So, tell me about Eric." Dale didn't actually want her to, but he wanted to keep up the appearance of being friendly. "Where did you two meet?"

"He's a secondary school teacher. We met at a bookstore, actually. He was returning a graphic novel he'd bought for his niece, and I was doing a signing. I was on a

4.4: The Name

break and we got chatting. That was almost five years ago now."

"Oh, cool... I'd have thought you'd have ended up with Owen."

Heather let out a frustrated sigh and shook her head, making her displeasure known without words. Owen used to work with her at Grovers, in their other life. Owen clearly fancied Heather at the time, though she'd never admit it. The two were friends and would occasionally go for a drink together. It was nothing – Dale trusted Heather, but every now and then the jealousy would bubble to the surface, and for a couple of years of their relationship it became a point of tension between them. It was much of nothing, but Dale bringing it up felt like an unfair dig. She decided not to bite back; she really didn't want to argue, and she'd been enjoying his company up until then.

"What about you, Dale? Is there someone special in your life?"

"There is, actually. I live with her. She's young, full of energy, mischievous..."

Heather raised an eyebrow. Was he now trying to make *her* jealous?

"Oh, and she's covered in fur. She's a cat."

"You got a cat?" Heather smirked.

"I did. A guy at work was moving to a place where they don't allow pets. I was meant to take her for a couple of weeks until he found something permanent, but that was three years ago now. There's no way anyone else is taking

4.4: The Name

her now. But no, I'm not with anyone. There's been a few, but they never really work out."

"Why not?"

Heather realised that Dale had stopped a few paces behind. She turned to see why; she could see his mind ticking over the question.

"Because they weren't you. It wasn't us." He shrugged.

The two began walking again, even slower than before. Their eyes flicked to a travel agent as they wandered past. There were postcards in the window promoting various holiday deals, one in particular catching their eye – a boat on a crystal-clear ocean. It was Tenerife, but it was enough to pull them both back to the memory of their time in Greece.

"Do you ever wish we could go back to that boat?" Heather asked. "You looking out over the ocean, me sunbathing with Lyndon, and we just enjoy the boat trip, visit a few islands, then go back to the mainland and depart as strangers?"

"No, not once, not ever." Dale didn't even need to think about it; he answered with certainty. "The universe showed us that day for a reason."

Their train of conversation was briefly disrupted by a *ding* sound in Heather's pocket. She shook it off.

"What reason?" she asked delicately.

Dale took hold of her arm, this time stopping them both. He looked deep into her eyes. On the surface, she seemed happy, content, but Dale could see the sadness behind the mask. This was his chance to talk to her, to *really* talk to her, to get through to her.

"Because you and I, we're *meant* to be together. I realise that now. That's why we saw what we saw. Something wanted us to know *how* good we could be together. We saw our destiny. We are *supposed* to be together."

Heather pulled away. "Goddamn it, Dale, not this again. Whatever we saw, we weren't supposed to see."

"Do you not love me?" he asked, unsure if he wanted to know the answer. "I guess always in all ways was a lie."

"Of course I love you. I have always loved you, Dale. I always will."

"And I love you. So why can't we be together?"

"I'm married!" She began walking away, this time with speed.

"I know, but so were *we*." He was doing his best to catch up with her.

Heather's cheeks began to turn a rashy red. Dale knew the colour well; it meant she was holding back tears. "We've been over this *so* many times, Dale. I'm sorry about what happened. You need to move on, you need a life of your own."

"I had a life, Heather. We had a life! Tell me something, are you happy?"

"I… I don't know how to answer that."

"We could *be* happy, Heather. Me and you."

4.4: The Name

There was another *ding* from Heather's pocket. She pulled out her phone, took a quick glance at the screen, then stuffed it back into her pocket.

"Shit, I'm sorry Dale, I've really got to go. I've gotta pick up my kid from school." She switched direction and walked with haste.

He followed after her.

"No, no, please, Heather, don't go! I'm sorry. Please." Dale began to panic.

"No, it's okay, it's okay, really, I just have to go." Her pace increased with each step.

"Shit, I've ruined it. I'm sorry, Heather."

"You haven't," she said, wiping another tear from her eye. She stopped for a second to allow him to catch up. "Honestly, Dale, it's not because of you. I have to go and pick him up, okay?"

"Well... maybe we could grab dinner or something later? Or tomorrow?"

"Yeah, maybe. I don't know." She began walking again, this time even faster, clearly trying to get away from the situation. "I just have to go get my son."

"I understand." Dale continued to follow her at speed. "What's his name?" he asked, attempting to keep the conversation going. He thought if he could bring it back to something more casual, maybe it would distract Heather from their uncomfortable interaction and the two could be friendly again.

"Who?"

4.4: The Name

"Your son, what's his name?"

"I'm sorry, Dale, I really have to go." Her footsteps quickened further.

"I know, I was just asking his name." Dale didn't really want to know, but he was starting to suspect she was avoiding the question.

"It doesn't matter," she said, continuing to wipe the occasional tear.

Dale caught up and turned to walk backwards in front of her, gently slowing her.

"Why won't you tell me his name?"

She stopped in her tracks. The rashy red spread over her entire face, neck, and arms in an instant, like a bulb lighting up, turning a shade darker than he'd ever seen it before. Tears began streaming down her face; she wasn't trying to stop them anymore. Her mouth didn't utter a word, but her face screamed an incomprehensible answer.

"No…" Dale said, the word wobbling as it left his mouth.

Heather's arms began to shake as her crying intensified. "Dale." She took his arm. "It's not like that."

"No, Heather, no, no, no!" Dale yanked his arm away and began pacing in fury.

"It's my grandfather's name, you know that, you know that it's a tradition that the first son of each generation takes the name."

Dale stared at her with anger in his eyes. "This is fucked up, Heather. This is seriously *fucked up*!"

4.4: The Name

"You think I don't know that?" she screamed. "You think it doesn't break my heart every time I call his name?"

"You named him! You fucking named him, Heather. How could you do this? How could you give him his name?"

Dale knees turned to jelly and he dropped to the floor, squeezing his head in his hands. His heart felt like it was wrapped in string, each strand pulling in a different direction, making it tighter and tighter until it was ready to burst.

"I'm sorry, Dale, I'm so sorry." Heather's face was soaked. She wasn't sure what to do with herself. She just stood in the street, staring at a man whose heart was breaking in front of her, unable to find the words to explain herself. Her arms were moving erratically, as if she'd lost control of them.

"This is so fucked up…" Dale repeated over and over.

"I tried, Dale, I really tried to fight the name. But you know what my parents are like. You know how seriously they take faith and traditions. You remember the fight you and I had with them, right? I almost lost them because of this, I was *ready* to lose them because of this! But… *we* didn't want him to grow up without his grandparents."

Dale lifted himself to his feet, every muscle in his body tightened.

"You replaced our son! Did Aiden mean so little to you that you just thought you'd have another one?"

Heather slapped Dale, hard, right across the face. When she realised what she'd done, she lunged forward and wrapped her arms around him, squeezing as hard as she could.

4.4: The Name

"I'm sorry, Dale. I'm sorry to my core. Please forgive me."

Dale pushed himself out of her embrace.

"You know what, Heather, I do wish I could go back to that boat. I wish I'd never met you. You've ruined my life."

He stormed away from her. He could hear her crying behind him, louder than he'd ever heard her before, but he didn't look back.

He wished he'd meant what he said. He wished he could hate her. Or, at the very least, he wished what she'd done was enough to stop him loving her. Shouldn't it be enough? What more could she do to hurt him? What more would it take?

4.5: The Game

Dale rushed up to his old bedroom the minute he returned to the family home. He grabbed handfuls of clothes from the floor and stuffed them back into his rucksack, then retrieved his toothbrush from the bathroom and threw it into the front pocket. His head felt like it was inflating. He wished he could grab a saw and take the top off his skull, just to relieve some of the pressure. How could she use his name? Was it a sign that, deep down, she wanted her old life back? Or was she really just so cold that her old life meant nothing?

There were other options, of course, but none occurred to Dale. Though on the surface he appeared relatively calm, his thoughts were spinning so fast they were jumbling into each other, making it impossible to really process any one of them. He'd always assumed that at some point Heather would come to her senses and realise they were meant to be together. But how long would he have to wait? How long would it take for her to understand as Dale did, that what they saw together was a guide for how their life was supposed to go? They'd been lucky enough to have been given a map, but she was choosing to ignore it.

Dale slung the bag over his shoulder and rushed down the stairs, not wanting to be in that house a minute longer than he had to. As he went to open the front door, someone else tried to open it from the other side at the same time. *Shit.* The door opened to reveal Jak returning to the family home.

4.5: The Game

"Jesus, Dale!" Jak was startled to see his brother on the other side of the door. "You scared the shit outta me."

Jak's eyes drifted upwards to see Dale clutching a bag over his shoulder. Suddenly, he realised what was happening.

"You were just going to go without saying goodbye?"

"I can't stay here, Jak."

"I take it things didn't go well with Heather then?"

Dale didn't respond. He didn't have to – Jak could see through his brother's expressionless mask to the pain hiding beneath.

"Shit. Well, I hate to say I told you so," Jak said. "Actually, no, I don't, I bloody love it." Jak smiled, but it wasn't returned. His attempt at lightening the situation had fallen flat. "Look, why don't you stay here, have a coffee, and we can talk about it."

"I can't." Dale stood to one side to let Jak come through the door. "It's clear there's nothing for me in New Oxford. Every time I come back here all I do is fight. *Always.*"

"What about when you're up north?" Jak removed his jacket and threw it over the banister.

"I feel like all I do there is fight too."

Jak sighed. "That's what happens when you're at war with yourself."

"Yeah, but up there I can handle it. Here…" Dale paused, his eyes shifting in their sockets. "You know what, it doesn't matter."

"Come on." Jak was intrigued. "Finish that thought."

4.5: The Game

"When I'm up north, I still feel like she's with me all the time. Like she's always standing behind me. It doesn't matter what I'm doing, driving to work, eating dinner, anything – I can feel her with me. I can feel *all* of them with me. But I've learnt to block it out, to live around it. I can *take* it. But when I'm here, in New Oxford, they're *all* so much louder that it's impossible to do anything else but think of them."

"This place was your home, Dale. It's bound to open old wounds."

"You have no idea." Dale's head dipped.

"Then tell me. Come on, help me understand." Jak ushered for Dale to move into the lounge behind them. It didn't work; he wouldn't take a single step. His feet were firmly planted by the exit, ready to escape.

"See that door?" Dale signalled towards the kitchen entrance. "Lynn was so excited on her sixth birthday that she ran into it and cut open her forehead. The TV in the lounge – Mum got mad at Aiden for leaving a big chocolate handprint right in the corner. She said she was never giving him chocolate again, but of course that didn't last long. The spare room upstairs, my old bedroom – that's where Heather and I had to stay for about a month during a move. We were going from a rented place into the first home we bought together, but it got delayed last minute, which meant we were stuck. *This* house, *this* city. I lived a whole life here. And now that's gone. When I see *her* it's like every cell in my body is on fire, but I don't know if it's a good fire or not. It's like there's too much to process. I miss her so fucking much,

4.5: The Game

Jak. I miss all of them. Aiden and Lynn are gone from my life, I know that. They didn't choose to be gone; it was out of all of our hands. But Heather is here, and she's *choosing* not to be with me. People keep telling me I need to move on, but they don't understand what it's like."

Dale exhaled with everything he had, like a balloon deflating. He didn't feel better for it, not really, but it relieved a tiny fraction of the pressure at least.

Jak clicked his tongue against the roof of his mouth, something he did when he was deep in thought, something Dale had always found incredibly annoying. Several times Jak went to speak, before pulling back at the last second. On the fourth attempt, he managed to dig out the words.

"Trauma like that," he said gently, "it shapes you. It sucks. It really shouldn't change you, but it just does. And you'll never be able to go back, to be unchanged. It's like… growing up, you're a ball of clay. When you're young, the things around you knock it and shape it. Some more than others. Then as you get older, that clay starts to harden, and all those dents and those cracks remain. What you went through, what you saw, Dale, your clay took one hell of a dent. And you've spent your whole life trying to fill that dent the only way that makes sense to you, and that's to find the missing piece and push it back in. But that's not how it works. You can't fill it in because it's not actually missing, it's just a different shape than before. An odd shape, of course, but nobody's clay is a perfect ball. So you can't fill it, you can't ignore it, you can't run away from it, and if you keep picking at it, then you're just gonna flake bits off and make it worse. I think the only way we ever really cope is to take a step back, look at our clay, and go, 'okay, that's my shape, how do I understand that? How do I live with that?'"

"How do *you* live with it?" Dale whispered.

"Me? I don't have that issue. My clay shape fucking rocks."

Dale gave a short burst of air from his nose, not quite enough to be considered a laugh. He resisted the urge to look at his brother's chair. "I don't mean *you* specifically... What should I do? None of this woolly 'learn to live with it' crap, I mean literal instructions. What do I do to solve this?"

Jak shrugged his shoulders. "You could start by getting angry. Not at anyone or anything in particular, just angry for the sake of it. That might help get it out of your system. Or just showing any sort of emotion. Have you got help? I mean, professional help? It helped me. It might be worth trying."

The question itself made Dale uncomfortable. He'd thought about trying it before, but how could anyone actually help him? What could anyone say to fix this?

"I think the best thing for me is to get out of New Oxford." Dale shuffled the bag back into the crook of his shoulder. He looked towards the front door, as if preparing to leave.

"Wait, Dale... Wait!" Jak thought quickly for a second. "I'll make you a deal. *Street Fighter*, best of three. If you win, you go home. If I win, you stay one more night."

"Why?" Dale pinched the bridge of his nose and pushed his eyes tight. He was tired, tense, with nothing left to give.

4.5: The Game

"Because I don't want whatever happened with Heather to be the end of your trip here. I don't want you to go back like this. Just spend the night, we'll order pizza and a couple of beers, and I promise I won't ask you what happened today."

Dale thought about it for a moment. He'd met his obligation to Jak, to his mother, and he had no reason to stay there any longer. Almost every part him just wanted to run away. *Almost.* There was a part that knew he had nothing to lose by staying. It would be a long drive home, and that was a lot of time for the day to fester in his head. He didn't want a distraction, but he knew he needed something to break him from the tension he felt in every part of his being.

"Fine, best of three," he said, "but if we're doing this, you're not allowed to be Blanka."

"Why not?" Jak laughed.

"Because you're just gonna do that zappy thing over and over."

"Fine." Jak smirked as he watched his brother put the bag onto the floor. "I don't need Blanka anyway. My legs don't work, Dale, but I'm still gonna kick your arse."

As night fell and the street turned dark and silent, one house was still ablaze with the artificial light of an outdated video game system. Inside, Dale and Jak were on the floor, surrounded by pizza boxes and discarded beer cans, sitting only inches away from the television. They were thirty-two matches into their best of three.

4.5: The Game

"You've definitely been practising." Dale slammed the controller down after yet *another* loss.

"Some of us are just talented." Jak raised his arms into a huge V, as if presenting himself, proud of his victory.

"Some of us are just spammy bastards."

The two of them laughed together. They'd laughed a lot that night.

"Dale," Jak said softly, "can I ask you something? In your... *thing*... when did Mum die?"

"Huh," Dale said, taken aback. It wasn't something he'd really thought about. "2007, I think."

"Well that's something, I guess. With me being here, she lived an extra three years."

"I guess so," Dale said, downing the remainder of his can. He grabbed another two from the last six-pack on the table and threw one over to his brother. He reclaimed his controller and began scrolling the character selection screen.

"Do we have to do this every time?" Jak said. "You spend ages searching just to pick Chun-Li again."

Dale shushed Jak and returned his gaze to the screen, flicking between the characters one at a time. He had something on his mind, but he knew if he looked at his brother, he'd be unable to say it. Instead, the tinny sound of the selection screen was keeping his mind distracted while he built up the courage.

"Jak... What you said, last night, at the pub..."

"Oh just ignore me. I'd had way too much to drink."

4.5: The Game

"No... no, you weren't wrong." Dale stared at the screen, a feeling of shame bubbling up inside him. "I think, maybe, I do blame you. I don't want to... I know it's not your fault. The accident wasn't your fault. Where the metal impaled you wasn't your fault. But you were right – you being here means they're not, and I can't shake that. I hate myself for it. I hate you for it, too. Does that make me a dick?"

"Yeah, it bloody does." Jak smiled – not the reaction Dale had expected. "It makes you a *massive* dick. But at least you're being honest. And *fuck it*, that's worth something."

Dale selected his character, Chun-Li, then held the controller firm, waiting for the distraction of the game to pull him away from the situation. Just as the match began and the two characters moved towards the middle of the screen ready to do battle, Jak hit the pause button and everything froze. They both kept their eyes on the screen, but Dale could sense his brother had something more to say.

Jak had to push every word through the lump in his throat. "If I could give up my life to bring them back to you, Dale, if I could go back to that car and move myself 1 mm more to the left, I would. In a heartbeat, *I would*."

"I know, Jak. I think I've always known."

Part 5
The Day
30 years after the vision

5.1: The Jacket

Dale sat on the edge of his bed, the rucksack by his feet stuffed with everything he owned – or everything he hadn't sold, anyway. The zipper was barely holding it together, ready to burst at any minute. Dale felt the same way, on edge with nervous anticipation for what was to come. The feeling made a nice change from the constant tiredness. He told himself that came from age, that being a man in his fifties was taking its toll, but he knew that wasn't it. He'd felt the same way for as long as he could remember – exhausted, lost, confused. But now it was different. Finally, there was an end in sight, and everything was about to change.

Still, in that moment of waiting, he began to feel the lethargy creeping in around the edges. This was the first time in weeks that he'd had a chance to just sit and stop; preparing for this day had kept him busy. His hair fell in front of his eyes as his head dipped forward. It was almost long enough to reach his beard, which was fuller than it had ever been before, reaching halfway down his hoodie. He'd been so focused on getting his life ready for the change that he hadn't had time to tidy himself up.

A knock came at the door, the one he'd been waiting for. He dragged his heavy rucksack through the hallway of his empty apartment and dropped it by the entrance.

"Louise," he said, as he answered the door. "Thanks for this."

5.1: The Jacket

"Hey Dale, long time no see!"

Louise looked a little different than Dale remembered. She still had striking red hair, but more of her natural roots had grown through than she'd usually allow, and the crow's feet around her eyes were a little more prominent than the last time he'd seen her. Neither was a negative – in fact, they suited her.

"Do you need anything before we go? A drink? Something to eat? Toilet?"

"I'm fine, I stopped about twenty minutes ago." Louise was already stepping backwards, clearly eager to leave.

Dale threw the rucksack over his shoulder, the force almost enough to knock him off his feet.

"Oh!" Louise said abruptly. "Don't forget the jacket."

"That fucking jacket!" Dale laughed. "I swear, he's text me about that every week since you here last, maybe three years ago? Every single *bloody* week. I offered to post the damn thing but he said no, he was worried it'd crease."

"I think he just wanted to make sure we saw you again."

Dale grabbed the leather jacket from the hook and wrapped it over his arm. He locked the door, then posted the keys back through the letterbox. The two of them carefully walked down the snowy staircase towards Louise's car. The snow hadn't stopped for almost a week. At any other time, Dale would have cancelled the trip, but he couldn't afford to wait – what needed to be done was now or never.

"He's far too old for this jacket now," Dale said as they reached the vehicle.

5.1: The Jacket

"He was too old when he bought it. But you know your brother, age never stops him from doing anything!" Louise jested. "Hey, hand it to me." She opened the boot and carefully placed the jacket inside. "I'm gonna tell him you forgot it."

"Make sure I'm not there when you do," Dale chuckled.

The two of them got into the car. Louise set up her phone as a satnav before starting the engine.

"So, your old car finally gave up then, Dale?"

"I ran that car for twenty years longer than I should have… I really appreciate you coming to get me today. I could have got the train or a taxi."

"One hundred and sixty miles in a taxi in the snow? That would have cost you a fortune!"

"To be honest, I wasn't sure you'd show. I know Jak doesn't approve of what I'm doing. Is that why he didn't come today?"

"No, not at all!" Louise insisted. "Somebody had to stay and look after Margaret. Who you still haven't met, by the way! We thought about bringing her, but trust me, you don't want to do this drive with a baby in the car. It would have driven you mad!"

"I remember those early years. From… you know. It's all crying, screaming, feeding…"

"Yeah, and that's just Jak!" Louise joked.

She dropped the handbrake ready to pull away but was struck with a moment of doubt. She reengaged the brake and took the car out of gear.

5.1: The Jacket

"Dale, are you certain about this? It's not too late to change your mind. Your work would take you back in a heartbeat, I know you loved it there. I'm sorry to ask again, I know Jak has…"

"Louise, I am 100% sure," he said, cutting her off. "I have no doubts. I've been stuck in limbo too long, but I finally understand it now. What it's all been for. You and Jak found your happiness. It's time for me to get mine."

"I just hope you know what you're doing."

Louise took a second to look deep into his eyes. He was unflinching; there was no changing his mind. She dropped the brake and pulled away.

Louise enjoyed the respite from her otherwise chaotic life. It was nice to have a few hours where nobody demanded anything of her, left with just the road and her thoughts. And Dale, of course, but he hadn't said much the whole trip, despite her efforts to engage him. The truth was his nerves were getting worse with each mile, and there were *so many* miles. He struggled with small talk at the best of times, but this was stretching his already-limited conversational response-pool. Before they knew it, the best part of three hours had disappeared.

"Hey, whatever happened to Gia?" Louise asked, casually trying one last attempt to take Dale's mind off the trip.

"Ah, that didn't last long. She thought she was just a rebound from my divorce and to be honest, I wasn't really invested."

5.1: The Jacket

"That's a shame. I really liked her."

Dale burst out laughing, Louise's comment having caught him off guard. For a moment it broke him from the nerves.

"She did not like you!" he said, smiling to himself.

"No, she did not. She didn't like your cats, either!"

"Did I tell you what she said after…" Dale stopped mid-sentence as something out the window caught his eye. Louise saw it too: the tired and rusted metal sign proudly displaying *Welcome to New Oxford*.

It all suddenly became much more *real*. Louise glanced at the man sitting next to her, his face falling into a look closely resembling dread. He was excited, of course, but at that moment those feelings were drowning in anxiety.

"How long has it been since you were last here?"

Dale thought back, trying to remember. "That was… our mother's funeral."

"Jesus, Dale! I didn't even know Jak then. That's like over ten years."

"Must be fifteen now."

"And you're sure you don't want to stay with us? We have the space. Margaret sleeps a solid two to three hours a night, so you'll get *some* rest."

"The hotel is fine."

"And you don't want me to take you back? When all this is done?"

Dale shook his head.

5.1: The Jacket

"There is no *done*. There is no *back* after tomorrow. Look, Louise, I don't know exactly how this is going to go, but I do know everything is about to change. This life, this one I'm not meant to have, it'll all be fixed tomorrow. Just do me a favour and look after Jak, okay?"

"I can't pretend to understand any of this Dale, but one thing I do know is that Jak and I will be here for you, whatever you need."

"Thank you. I'm glad you two found each other."

"I'm just glad you found his jacket!"

5.2: The Razor

Dale stared at himself in the hotel mirror. When did he get so old? When did he get so hairy? He took the rusted scissors from his wash bag and began chopping at the long mass on his head. There was no precision to his movements, no care or pattern, he just grabbed whatever he could with one hand and cut it away with the other. Within seconds, the yellowed sink of his dingy hotel room was full of his offcuts. Once the majority had gone, he slowed and took more care as he attempted to even it out. He was no barber, but he managed to do a decent-enough job of getting his hair back to its former self. Back to how it was when he used to take better care of himself. He ruffled what little hair was left, then took a good look.

Why did the hair of his younger self make him somehow look *even* older? The mishmash of his youthful hair with his aged face didn't sit right. But he wasn't done – he picked up the scissors again and carefully snipped at the long strands of hair sticking from his nose. Next were ears, then eyebrows. Finally, he reached his beard. He couldn't remember when he was last clean shaven. This was the part he was dreading. Without his beard, he looked like his other self, and that self carried too many painful memories. But that was the self he needed for what was coming. Shaving the beard was a means to an end. *The* end. The everything.

He squirted some shaving cream into his hand and lathered his face the best he could, working it through his

5.2: The Razor

long, scraggly beard. He took out his old razor, one that hadn't been used in years, and rinsed it under the hot tap. He gently dragged the blades down his left cheek. It moved less than an inch or two before getting matted in the overlong hair. He pulled harder, attempting to free it, but all it did was snap the handle in half, clearly grown brittle from all the years of disuse.

Shit.

He sifted through his wash bag, hoping he had a spare, but he knew he didn't. He then checked all the cupboards in the bathroom, hoping the hotel might have provided one. It soon became obvious his hopes were in vain. He rinsed the foam from his face and beard, then took a good look in the mirror, wincing at his new bald patch. He considered his options – leaving it that way was out of the question, so the only viable option was to get a replacement. Maybe two… three, just to be sure. After pacing the room and swearing to himself, he threw on his hoodie and left the hotel into the darkness of the night.

Just around the corner, less than half a mile walk, was Appleberrys. It was slightly bigger than your typical corner shop, but not quite enough to be considered a supermarket. It was just the right size to carry what Dale needed. The inside was brightly lit with sharp white lights, like a sterile hospital office. It was enough to make Dale squint as he wandered the store. Once his eyes had adjusted, he checked the signs above the aisles before making a beeline for the toiletries.

5.2: The Razor

There were all sorts of men's razors, with lubricating strips, extra trimming blades, or ergonomic handles designed for precision. He didn't need any of that, he just needed the beard gone. He grabbed a pack of five cheap plastic razors from the bottom shelf. Out of nowhere, the hairs on the back of his neck stood on end – someone was behind him.

"Dale?"

He stood and turned to see a woman standing in the middle of the aisle holding an empty basket. She was tall with long blonde hair, early fifties he thought, around the same age as him. He didn't recognise her.

"Dale, it *is* you. How have you been?"

He scanned her face, waiting for his memory to tell him who she was.

"It's me, Suzanne. We dated for a few months when we were younger."

"Suzanne!" It all came flooding back. It was her, the girlfriend he went to Greece with all those years ago. He began to see features he recognised, the youthful face under this older mask. "Of course. Sorry, I was miles away."

"Shaving accident?" she said, pointing to her cheek as if to signal his.

"Oh, yeah." Dale became self-conscious about the bald patch. "The razor snapped. I've just come to get more."

"You don't want to razor *that* beard, Dale. No blade is going to get through that. Trust me, use an electric shaver to cut away most of it before you use the razor."

5.2: The Razor

"Oh... thanks." Dale nodded – that did sound sensible. He made a note to himself to pick up a shaver before he left. "So how are you, Suzanne? Are you still a... umm... sportswriter?"

"Sort of. I started my own magazine about a decade ago. I thought I'd get to write more of my own stuff that way, but it seems to be the opposite. I end up doing the admin, and other people get to do the fun writing bits! Oh, and I just moved. I bought a place over on Nether Avenue."

Dale's ears pricked. "I grew up there. Right next to the cool field."

"The what?"

He grinned to himself; he'd said it so casually. He was struck with a wave of bitter-sweet nostalgic memories, the joy of remembering those times accompanied by the sadness that they had long since passed. He hadn't thought about the cool field in years.

"Never mind, it was an old bike field that was there."

"That's still there, I live opposite. 'The cool field', I'll have to start calling it that!"

Dale shuffled on the spot, unsure of what to say.

"What about you, Dale?" she asked. "How are you? How's your life?"

"I'm good, I'm..." The sadness struck harder. Seeing her, thinking of the cool field, it all reminded him of life before the vision, a life that was so much simpler, where he didn't feel like he was missing half of himself. It was too much to take at once. He had to quickly counter the weight the only

5.2: The Razor

way he knew how – by slipping into a comforting lie. "Do you remember that Heather woman? The one we met on the boat? Well, we're married."

"No way!"

"Yeah. We, uh, we got home after that holiday, and we talked about, you know, what we saw, and we decided to give it a go. And luckily, it all worked out. We've been together getting on thirty years now. We've got two amazing kids, Aiden and Lynn."

"That's wonderful, Dale. It sounds like you've had a good life." Her smile was genuine.

"I've been very lucky."

Suzanne's eyes dropped, her tone softening. "That *thing*… with the boat… and all that. I've always felt a bit guilty for leaving the way I did."

"No, no, you've no reason to. It was a lifetime ago."

"Well, you were obviously going through something, and I just kinda left you to it. But I'm glad it all worked out for you both."

"The whole thing was so weird," Dale said.

Suzanne smiled from cheek to cheek. "Just imagine how different life would've been if we'd gone for the quad bikes!"

The two paused for a moment, neither sure how to react.

"Anyway," Suzanne said awkwardly, clearly wanting to continue her evening, "sorry but I've gotta rush. It was nice seeing you, Dale."

5.2: The Razor

"Yeah, you too. See you around sometime."

Dale allowed himself a rare moment of reflection, contemplating how his life would have been different if they'd never got on that boat. Would he ever have met Heather? Would… He told himself it was all pointless to consider. There was a reason, a purpose, an intention to what happened. They *did* get on that boat, and his hand *did* touch Heather's, and the two of them *did* experience a full day together in an alternate future.

That day was November 18th, 2025.

That day was tomorrow.

5.3: The Touch

Dale took a deep breath, perhaps the deepest he ever had. He'd worked his notice, sold his apartment, rehomed the cats, and closed down all remnants of his life. His old life. He was back in a city he'd twice called home. The day he'd been waiting for had finally arrived, the day that his time in his wrong life would end, and everything would return to what *should* have been.

Finding her address had been much easier than he'd expected. Heather wasn't one to post much on social media, but there was one picture of her three kids where she'd tagged William, her third husband. Looking at his profile revealed a few mutual friends, people Dale knew from when he used to live in the area. One of them owed Jak a favour, and Dale leveraged that (much to Jak's disapproval) to get Heather and William's address. The hard part of the last few weeks had been resisting the urge to just go and see her, but he knew it had to be today.

Dale didn't waste a moment. As soon as the sun rose, he threw on his hoodie and jeans, then called a taxi. He'd been tempted to wear something a little more formal, something smart, but that didn't feel right. This was about returning to his normal life, his *proper* life, and he needed to do that in the way he'd spent most of it. His hair was back to its old self, or as close as he could get it, and he was clean shaven (thanks to Suzanne's tip). He was ready. He hadn't slept a wink; his heart churned and his nerves pumped

5.3: The Touch

adrenaline into every fibre of his body. The feelings only intensified as his taxi approached its destination.

He stood opposite the house. The morning was grey, sitting just on the edge of rain. Dale had hoped the snow would reach New Oxford before he did, the cold making it all easier, but sadly he'd beaten it. He watched the house, his heart thumping so hard he could hear it, as he searched for the courage to do what needed to be done. He saw the curtain twitch, and a face stared directly at him.

"Shit," he mumbled to himself, disappointed that the timing had been taken out of his hands.

He recognised the face from the pictures online – William. They knew Dale was there now; there was no more waiting. It was time.

The front door swung open before Dale even reached it. William stood tall, blocking the porchway, his chest puffed out. Heather stood just behind him.

"Go away," William said sternly. There was an aggression in his voice.

"Heather, I need to talk to you." Dale's words floated past the man in the doorway.

"I know who you are. She's told me all about it. You need to—"

"Will, stop!" Heather commanded, before turning her attention to Dale, her eyes soft, sympathetic. "You need to go home, hun."

5.3: The Touch

"Do you know what day it is?"

"Of course I do, Dale. I expected you to come today. I hoped you wouldn't. I *really* hoped you wouldn't, but I knew you would."

"I just need two minutes to talk to you," Dale pleaded. "Just two minutes, then I'll be gone."

As they spoke, three children took turns to poke their heads around a door from inside the house to see what was going on. William noticed.

"You're scaring the kids. Just get lost," he said.

Heather turned and ushered the kids into the lounge, then closed the door and returned to Dale.

"Heather, please," Dale said, "we just have to touch. That's all. Just one touch and everything will be right again." William flexed his arms and stepped closer to the man at his door, ensuring there was a barrier between him and Heather.

"Fuck off, now. You're not touching my wife."

"William, stop!" Heather shouted. "You're making it worse. Go inside."

"I'm not leaving you with him!"

"Yes, you *are*. Now go!"

William glared at Dale, making sure he knew how unimpressed he was to see him there. After a few moments of attempted intimidation, William reluctantly left Dale and went to join the kids in the lounge.

"You and I, we're in the wrong life," Dale said, taking a step toward her.

5.3: The Touch

"Don't, Dale. Step back." She put her arms up, signalling him to stay away.

He considered rushing her, forcing her to touch him, but he didn't want to return to their *proper* life that way.

"This," Dale signalled to the house, to the lounge door, "this isn't how things are meant to be. The universe showed us today for a reason. Today! It wasn't just random. I understand what that reason is now. Today is the day that it wants us to come together again. If we touch, like we did on that boat, everything will go back to normal. We'll get back to Lynn and Aiden, to me and you. All we have to do is touch, and we can get it all back."

Tears began to form in Heather's eyes, though she just about managed to hold them back. "No, Dale... no. It won't work. It won't do anything."

"Then why don't you touch me and see? Don't you miss them?"

"Of course I do." Her grip on the tears loosened; they fell in a stream faster than she could catch them.

"Doesn't it feel like they should be here? Don't they feel real?"

"As real as the stars."

"Then touch my hand. That's all I ask. We can get them back." Dale's eyes widened in desperation. He just needed her to see what had to be done.

"Dale, nothing will happen..."

"But if you think that, then—"

5.3: The Touch

She interrupted him. "*Nothing* will happen. But even if somehow it did, I'd lose as much as I gain. Always in all ways, Dale. But you need to go home now. I'm hoping that after today has gone, you'll find some way to move on from this."

"Touch my hand, Heather." Dale pulled back his sleeve and presented his hand. "Just touch it and see. We'll go right to this day. You'll be preparing dinner, I'll be doing the cleaning, and they'll be on their way to us."

William burst through the door behind them.

"I've had enough of this!" he shouted. "You've upset my wife, you've scared the kids, and I've asked you to leave nicely."

He leapt forward and pushed Dale's chest, making him fall backwards into the street.

Heather grabbed her husband's arm. "What the hell are you doing?"

He didn't react, his eyes laser-focused on Dale. "The police are on the way. I just called them," William shouted, much to Heather's disapproval.

"William, for God's sake! Why did you do that? Dale isn't a threat. Just leave us to it."

Dale got up from the floor and stared at William, his mind searching for an appropriate reaction.

"Dale, don't!" Heather said, fearing he may try to push him back.

5.3: The Touch

"Just touch my hand, Heather. You'll see. All this pain, all this anger, it will just disappear. Everything will go back to normal."

"Everything *is* normal, Dale. I'm sorry things didn't work out how you wanted, but that's life. Us touching won't change anything."

"Then why won't you do it, huh? I know why – because you're scared of what will happen when I'm right."

"No, Dale!" she shouted. "I'm scared of what will happen when you're wrong!"

William clenched his fist. "You've got two minutes to—"

"Stop, just stop, both of you!" Heather grabbed her husband's hand firmly, as if to assert her dominance over the situation. "Go and look after the kids, please. I will sort this out."

"I'm not leaving you with him again."

"Just…" She glanced over William's shoulder to see a New Oxford Constabulary car coming around the corner. "Damn."

The police car stopped just short of Dale, red-faced and brushing himself off in the middle of the road. A young woman in uniform stepped out of the car.

"Heather, everything okay here?" the officer asked. She clearly knew Heather well. Dale surmised that Heather, being a semi-famous author, was probably no stranger to unwanted attention. He guessed this wasn't the first time the police had been called to the address to remove unwanted guests.

5.3: The Touch

"We're fine, thanks, June." Heather's voice carried with it an annoyance that the police were now involved in the situation.

"We're not fine," William snapped. "This man is harassing us."

"I'm her husband... ex-husband. But that will change as soon as she touches me." Dale suddenly became aware of how nuts he sounded saying it out loud.

The officer walked over to Dale and softly placed her hand on his back.

"Come on," she said, "let's leave these people to their day."

Her hand became firmer as she guided him towards the vehicle. With each step, Dale became more and more aware that his plan was failing.

"Heather, please, just touch my hand. Just once, and all this will be fixed."

His panic intensified, his arms beginning to shake. This wasn't working. How could she not see what needed to happen? Worse, why did she not want to fix this?

"Heather, please! It must be today. Don't do this, Heather, don't do this!"

Tears coated almost every part of her face. She had never seen Dale like this before, so desperate, so scared that he was losing it all.

The officer opened the back door to the police car and began urging Dale towards it, gently at first but becoming more of a push as he resisted.

5.3: The Touch

"Don't do this, Heather! You're killing our children! You're killing Lynn and Aiden. Don't let them die!"

Dale's knees gave way as he fell onto the back seat of the car. He sat himself upright and fixed his gaze on Heather. How could he convince her? Why wouldn't she do it? Why, why, *why*?

The officer closed the door, then moved around to the front seats.

"Wait!" Heather rushed towards Dale.

"Heather, don't!" her husband shouted.

"Just go back inside, William. Stop getting involved."

Heather approached the back of the car.

"Are you sure about this?" the officer asked, preparing to join her. Heather put her hand up as if to stop her.

She closed her eyes and took a deep breath, then opened the car door.

Dale's face lit up – this was the moment he'd been waiting for.

"I'm sorry for this, Dale. Always in all ways, please remember that," Heather said. She leant forward and stretched her hand out to meet his. The tips of her fingers brushed the palm of his hand, just ever so slightly. As their skin touched, everything went dark – pitch black in an instant, like a light bulb suddenly blowing out.

This was it; this was what everything had been leading to. He could hardly contain his excitement. He was ready to greet his new life. His other life. His *real* life.

5.3: The Touch

Dale slowly opened his eyes. There she was, his beautiful wife, standing in front of him, just like he knew she would be. But something wasn't right. She was upset, tears rolling down her cheeks. She was in the street, but Dale was… he was in a car? A police car?

Suddenly, it hit him.

Nothing had changed.

He grabbed hold of Heather's hand and squeezed it. He turned it over, grabbed it with the other hand, lifted her sleeves, tried touching parts of her arms, but there was nothing. As she pulled her hand away, Dale's excited face faded into heartbreak. It hadn't worked. He had been wrong about the day. He had been wrong about everything.

He was speechless, his mind erased. Whatever happened next did so in silence for Dale. At some point the door must have closed, the engine must have started, the car must have pulled away. It was all a blur. Time felt off in a way he couldn't grasp, like a slow-motion movie on fast forward.

How could he have been so wrong? How could it all have been for nothing? Whatever happened between him and Heather on that boat was a one-time thing, and now, after all these years, he realised that they were never meant to be. Not in this life.

5.4: The Clay

What could have been?

The question haunted Dale as they walked him through the station. They asked him his name, his address, what he was doing at the author's house... but he couldn't speak. What could he possibly say that would make any sense? His eyes were fixed on nothing, glazed over and vacant. When they touched, everything was supposed to slot into place again. The world was meant to go bright; they were meant to wake up in their bed, excited for their kids to visit today. But, for the second time in his life, it had been robbed from him. He was a shell.

His whole *lives* flashed before his eyes, an infinite number of opportunities and paths that were taken from him. Or, as he knew deep down, paths he'd denied for himself. But that truth was too much to bear.

What could have been?

What if he and Suzanne had gone on the quad bikes? They would have missed the boat trip. Maybe the rest of the holiday would have strengthened them as a couple. Maybe they would have stayed together, even got married one day. Maybe Anna would have been his best man. Maybe he and Suzanne would have spent their whole lives together. Or maybe one of them would have cheated. Maybe they would have ended up divorced. Maybe he would only see their kid on the weekends and holidays.

5.4: The Clay

Or maybe they would have broken up in Greece anyway. Maybe he, without the resentment he held for Jak, would have gone into business with him. Maybe the two of them would have taken over their mother's company. Maybe working together, with a bit of brotherly competition, would have pushed them both harder. Maybe they would have grown the business into something far bigger than their mother ever would have dreamt.

Or maybe he would have moved away anyway. Maybe he would have moved abroad. Or maybe not. Maybe he and Anna would have opened their own waffle cafe. Or maybe he would have gone to work for boring Bob. Or maybe he would have invented something new, or written something, or painted something, or become an astronaut, or a dancer, or a life coach. Or maybe he would have used the money from his mother's estate to buy Harman's construction firm and fully embrace his career as a health and safety consultant. Maybe he could have actually followed through with that plan instead of feeling like he was constantly being called to a life that didn't exist. Maybe he would have done something. Maybe he would have done *something*! Maybe he would have had a life of his own. Maybe he wouldn't have wasted it. Maybe he would've felt complete. Maybe he would have been happy.

Or not numb, at least.

A cacophony of overlapping *maybes* consumed every part of his being, so much so that he was barely able to process his surroundings. He knew he was alone in some sort of overly bright soft interview room at the station, and he vaguely heard the mumbles from the officers before they left.

5.4: The Clay

But none of that mattered. As the maybes subsided, they gave way to a much darker chain of thoughts.

What was the point of the vision?

What was the point of his life?

What *is* the point of his life?

Everything he ever wanted was gone, and now he knew it would never return. *They* would never return. He had wasted his life, and nobody would ever understand why. He was truly alone.

What does he do now?

What does he have left?

"Dale? Daaaaale?"

The light flickered, just enough for his eyes to adjust to what was in front of him – a hand, waving right in his face, trying to get his attention.

"You there?" the soft voice said.

Dale lifted his head the best he could. When had it gotten so heavy? He could just about make somebody out in front of him. They weren't in uniform, though – they were in hoodie and jeans, like him.

"Oi Dale! Wake up, you weirdo," the figure shouted.

The voice caused neurons to fire in his brain and activate his memory centres. "Anna?" She looked older. She looked different. No... she looked exactly the same.

"Oh, you are alive then," she said. "I'm not even meant to be here today. Heather called the station and told them to find me. So, here I am."

5.4: The Clay

"Heather called you? It's over... me and her, it's really over."

"Yeah, I know." Her voice carried genuine sympathy.

Dale began to snap back into life. As he did, his mind refocused onto something else. "Anna, I'm so sorry. I *really* let you down, didn't I? All those years ago."

"Yeah. You were a bloody idiot. Wanna make it up to me?"

"How?"

Anna winked. "Buy me breakfast."

Just a short walk from New Oxford's city centre, down a tired dilapidated alleyway, was Waffle On. The tiny cafe was the only thing on the street left open. It was easy to miss, and even those who spotted it tended to steer clear. Waffles and coffee were the only things on the menu, but that was all it needed. The outdated chalkboard, barely managing to stay propped up on the street outside, shouted about how cheap the place was in poorly drawn bubble letters. It didn't claim the food was *good*, but cheap was exactly what had first drawn Anna and Dale to the place years ago when they were teenagers.

And now, sitting at a table they hadn't shared in almost thirty years, the duo of once best friends basked in the warm nostalgic joy of a place that once meant so much to them. The tables were still just as sticky, the walls as tired, the smell as burnt, but they wouldn't have it any other way.

5.4: The Clay

Anna watched as Dale coated his waffle in syrup. She began to wonder at what point the ratio of waffle-to-syrup tipped in favour of the latter; she suspected it was a jug or two ago. It was a sight she hadn't seen in *so* long, that golden river that carried with it so many happy and formative memories.

Waffle On looked exactly the same now as it did when Dale left. It looked exactly the same now as when they were teenagers. That was part of the charm, they told themselves.

"Are you okay, Dale?" It was a pointless question – she knew he wasn't okay, but she needed to break the silence.

"No, I'm not. Not really. My entire life has been a waste. I feel like I've been a ghost, waiting to wake up back in my body, but now I never will. I've lost them. I mean, really lost them this time. I've lost her," he replied, barely looking at her.

She thought for a second... a minute... a couple of minutes. "Can I tell you a story, Dale?"

He shrugged.

"I've spent almost my entire life with Bob, over thirty years with the same man. He has stuck with me through so much, more than I could possibly tell you in one day, and I've stuck with him the same. We haven't always had a great life – there were times when things have been challenging, times when I wasn't sure we'd make it. But they always balanced out with the good. Things always got better. I have had a truly wonderful life. I have so many beautiful memories. All those years together, they're just memories, that's all they are now. I can replay them in my mind, I can

5.4: The Clay

keep them alive by sharing them with others, but I can never experience them again. Yet, those memories were my life, they were my everything. And that got me thinking. What if I went to bed tonight, then woke up tomorrow morning back in my twenties, and Bob wasn't there?"

Dale lifted his head; the last line struck him.

Anna continued, "Do you know what the very first thing I'd do is? I'd find my husband, without *any* hesitation. And if he said no, if he said he didn't want to be together anymore, and I was going to have to face a life without him... Well, I don't think I could ever stop asking."

For the first time, maybe in his entire life, Dale cried. The floodgates opened, and he began to sob uncontrollably, his shoulders bouncing as he struggled to hold it back. He cried, and cried, and cried. Finally, after all this time, all this heartache, all this pain, he was seen.

Anna reached across the table and held his hand, smiling at someone who once meant more to her than the world.

"Is it the thought of being stuck with Bob for thirty years that's made you like this?" she joked.

Dale laughed through the tears. He grabbed the napkin from under his plate and used it to dry his eyes the best he could. As he looked back up, he saw Anna sitting opposite him, an old familiar smile on her face. This time he saw her, he *really* saw her. He felt more relaxed in that moment than he had in the last thirty years. He'd been so focused on what had happened, so distracted, so obsessed, that it hadn't really hit him just how much he missed her. He *really* missed

5.4: The Clay

her. He was a mess without her. Jak had been wrong; Dale did have a piece of clay missing.

It was her.

He squeezed her hand a little tighter.

"I know things haven't worked out how you wanted," she said quietly, "but at least you're here now." Her voice got a little louder as she continued. "Hell, just think, if you'd stayed with Suzanne, you wouldn't even be alive right now."

The corner of Dale's mouth twisted. His mind was too tired to work out what she was referring to.

"Because she would have killed you… with an axe."

"She wasn't an axe murderer!"

The two laughed together and Dale felt the tension releasing from his bones.

"You know, Anna, you've never once asked me where you were in, you know, my *other* life. Whenever I told people what I saw, after the initial feigned sympathy, they'd ask me what *they* were doing, what *their* life was like. But you never did."

Anna shrugged her shoulders.

"Some things we just aren't meant to know," she said with certainty. "If you'd have told me what you saw about me, my life would have been loaded with expectation. I saw you, Dale. I saw how heavy that was to carry. I saw what knowing something like that does. I thought about asking you, I thought maybe it would have shared your burden, but it wouldn't. I believe it would have doubled it."

5.4: The Clay

"Well, it doesn't matter now anyway," he said. "This is the day we saw. I don't have other-life memories beyond this point."

"Oh... well, in that case, it can't do any harm. What was I like then?"

"Honestly," Dale said, "you were exactly like you are now. You were a police officer, and you and Bob were together, just the two of you. You had a good life."

"Huh, well ain't that something." She smiled contentedly to herself. "What about us? Me and you? Were we friends?"

Dale felt his eyes well up again. He tried to hold back but thinking about his other life was too much. He wiped the few that ran free.

"Yeah, we were," he whispered. "*Best* friends."

The two of them ate their waffles in relative silence. It wasn't awkward, it wasn't uncomfortable, neither expected the other to talk, neither was waiting for the conversation to start. They just sat and enjoyed a true moment of stillness.

"Oh, guess what?" Anna said excitedly. "Bob collects model trains now."

Dale laughed, wobbling his head in playful disbelief. "No he doesn't."

"I shit you not. He has a full-on train track built around the inside of our garage. It's got hedges and bridges and these tiny little people and all sorts. I am not even joking; he has spent *hundreds* of pounds building that thing. Sometimes he'll be in there for half the weekend. He even has a little conductor hat."

5.4: The Clay

"Now I know you're lying!"

"I swear to God. Come to dinner at ours tonight and I'll show you."

Dale smiled. "I'd like that."

Also available – another New Oxford Novella
Kris Crossing

Plagued by the tragedy of her past, local celebrity Hollie Crossing has disappeared. Though her mother and boyfriend do everything they can to find her, their worst fears are confirmed when Hollie's jacket is found in a river... She has taken her own life. Meanwhile, 300 miles across the country, Kris Gibson is a struggling drug addict looking for any opportunity to get clean and make something more of her life. Everything is a struggle for Kris, as she begs and steals just to survive the day. When Kris comes into possession of a wallet belonging to the missing Hollie Crossing, she takes on her identity, using it to put herself on a path to recovery. Things, however, are not as simple as they seem, and Kris begins to notice changes that she can't explain…

Printed in Great Britain
by Amazon